Something Old

AN AGE GAP, FORCED PROXIMITY, MAFIA ROMANCE

FAMILIA VECE
BOOK 2

HANNAH RIO

CHAPTER ONE
Masaccio

I stride into the venue with a sour look on my face.

I am not a fan of weddings and if I had a choice, I would definitely be somewhere else.

I'm a bit late. I hate being late. But there was an issue at the warehouse, and I had to see to it at the last minute.

It looks like the entire wedding is running behind schedule, anyway.

Typical.

These things never happen on time.

I take a seat on the bride's side of the church benches. My cousin, Isabella, has been talking nonstop about her wedding today.

"Mas, where the hell have you been?" the urgent voice comes from behind me, a hand on my shoulder. "Isabelle is so annoyed that you weren't here on time."

I turn to face my sister, Dalila. She is dressed in a bridesmaid's dress and seeing her reminds me I am actually a groomsman. Shit.

"Oh fuck. I forgot I was supposed to be a part of the ceremony." I roll my eyes and stand up. Dalila shakes her head, grabs my arm, and starts dragging me out of the church.

"Go and talk to the other groomsmen. They are all getting ready in the hotel across the street." She shoves me in the direction I need to go.

Without a word, I hurry across the road.

It's a quiet little town just outside of the city. Peaceful, pretty, old world style living.

When I arrive at the hotel, the party of groomsmen is already down in the lobby.

I walk straight over to my cousin's about-to-be-husband. "Frankie, I'm so sorry I'm late, man."

"Don't stress about it at all. You missed out on a few shots of tequila, but nothing much else. The exciting stuff is about to happen now." He shakes my hand, a massive smile on his face. He looks eager, like he's thrilled about getting married today.

I don't get it.

I don't get what all the fuss is about.

Marriage looks like a lot of hard work, a lot of stress. It's just to time consuming having to worry constantly about another person like that.

Well, I'm happy for Isabelle.

Frankie straightens the collar of my shirt, even though it's already straight.

I hold back the urge to brush his hand away. I don't like being touched.

"Dante, hand me one of those - perfect - yes. Thank you."

He neatly places a piece of folded cloth and a single rose into the top pocket of my jacket. Now I match the rest of the guys. A dark maroon rose against an olive-green square.

I smile. "Thanks. Looks good."

"You ready?" he asks.

"Are you ready?" I ask with a chuckle. From my point of view, he is about to throw his entire life away.

"I've never been more ready for something in my entire life." He really is fucking happy about this. I smile again, thinking about the dread I would feel if this was my wedding day.

Nope.

Not for me.

The groomsmen push through the doors of the hotel, out onto the streets. They are chatting and happy for Frankie. I'm happy for him too. He's a good guy and my cousin deserves a good guy.

I follow them into the church where the guests are getting agitated with the wait.

Frankie walks up the aisle with his groomsmen in tow. He speaks loudly when he greets everyone. "Hi, hello, it shouldn't be long now." He laughs.

But when he gets to the podium, standing - ready and waiting - he looks a little pale in the cheeks.

"What's wrong?" I lean forward and ask him.

"What if she changes her mind? What if I say something wrong or mess up my vows? What if something goes wrong—" he is shifting from foot to foot.

I grab his shoulder in a firm grip. "That girl loves you, man. Even if you messed up every word of your vows, she would marry you. Enjoy this moment."

He nods, the smile returning to this face, despite his nerves. "You're right. Thanks."

The church organ plays, and every single person turns towards the doors to watch Isabelle walking into the church.

I admit, she looks amazing. And even though this really isn't my scene at all, a fond, warm smile steals its way onto my face.

The ceremony is in full swing, and I feel like I've been standing for hours. I'm bored as fuck.

The bridesmaids are all lined up on the opposite side of the podium, and one of them, in particular, keeps staring at me.

Leora Alesso.

The daughter of Marco Alesso, a rival to my father and my family. Which makes Leora a rival by default. But Isabelle and Leora went to college together and because we all live in the same city, we inevitably end up hanging out in the same social circles.

She keeps watching me, a mischievous smirk on her face.

I make a point of not returning the stare.

She is trouble.

Daddy's little princess who gets whatever she wants whenever she wants it. A brat. Spoilt and entitled. Besides, despite being stunning, I wouldn't touch her - her father is so strict about her dating life. I reckon he'd kill any man who made a move.

It doesn't stop her from throwing herself at men. She loves the attention.

The priest is droning on and on about love and commitment. Fuck. Will this nightmare ever end? I need a drink and some food.

Staring over Leora's head and trying to ignore the wink she throws me, I breathe a sigh of relief when the priest says *I now pronounce you husband and wife.* Finally.

The bride and groom walk out hand in hand, and each bridesmaid and groomsman partners together and follows behind them.

Of course - I fucking get stuck with Leora.

She slips her arm through mine as we walk. "Hi Masaccio. You look really sexy." She grins up at me with those caramel eyes. Bright and full of suggestion. Her lips are painted a soft fudge color, perfectly outlined. Dark lashes frame her gaze.

For a moment, I can't look away.

"Leora." I clear my throat, turning my head forward again.

I could tell her she looks incredible. She does. That dark olive-green dress compliments her eyes and hugs her body in the most perfect way.

But if I say that, it will only encourage her flirtatious behavior. I'll enjoy the view silently, rather.

As soon as we are out of the church, I pull my arm away from hers.

The show is over.

I can get a drink now.

I walk away from the bridal party towards the reception hall. Getting annoyed with Leora follows me. I turn around to confront her.

"I think you should stay with your friends." I snap.

"Mm. Maybe you didn't get the memo, Mas, but you and I are paired up for the entire night. There are dances, and speeches and photographs - every groomsman is paired with a bridesmaid - and you and I are basically on a date tonight."

I shake my head. "We are *not* on a date, Leora. And right now, I need a moment alone. You can find me when I have groomsmen duties."

She grabs my arm.

"Right now, actually, it's time for the photographs." Leora says.

She giggles as she pulls me in the opposite direction of the bar. For fuck sakes. Are you kidding me right now?

I sigh and walk with the rest of the group towards the photographer.

It's going to be such a fucking long day.

Leora is all over me. Her arm slipped through mine again as she leans into me as though we are long lost lovers. I remain stiff. Not responding to her touch delisted the fact that having such a beautiful girl this close to me is causing a physical reaction in my body.

I'll just have to get over it.

Nothing good will come of giving in to Leora Alesso's advances.

CHAPTER TWO
Leora

The reception is thrumming with music and people talking and loud laughter. Everyone is in an incredible mood and enjoying the celebrations - everyone - that is - except my date.

Masaccio has always been such a serious looking, brooding type of guy. Technically, I should view him as boring as all hell - but he's so freaking hot. And being the sexiest guy, I've ever met in my life - it makes his dark, bad-boy attitude irresistible.

I stand up from the table where we are seated together for the bridal party and reach out to grab his hand. "Come dance with me." I say, pulling at him. He doesn't budge. He throws me the same stern look he's been giving me all night.

I grin, ignoring it. "Dance with me, Mas." I say again, batting my eyelashes at him.

He rolls his eyes, and I watch the muscles along his jaw feather.

Dammit. So sexy.

"I don't dance." Mas replies.

"Don't be silly, Mas, dance with the girl." Isabelle looks up from a conversation she was having with Frankie. The newlyweds look so happy tonight. My heart explodes with jealously that they found each other. I turn my attention back to Mas. He can't say no to the bride's request.

"Fine." He says gruffly, standing up. He's so much taller than me I have to tilt my head almost all the way back to look up at him. He's taller than almost everyone at this wedding.

He walks ahead of me towards the dance floor, not holding my hand or even bothering to check if I'm following him.

I am, though.

On the dance floor, he turns towards me, and I step close to him to wrap my arms around his neck. His hands slip around my waist, leaving heated trails on my skin where he touches me.

I've never been with a man before. I've never even kissed a guy. My father would lock me in a room and throw away the key if I even talked about something like that.

My father is so hell bent on keeping me *untouched* and *perfect*.

He never lets me have any fun. I'm not even allowed to go on chaperoned dates.

But tonight - at the wedding - well it would be rude of me not to dance with *my* groomsman. Besides, my father isn't here. This is the wedding of a rival family. I'm only here because Isabelle and I have been friends forever. And it took a huge amount of convincing to get my father to agree to let me come.

At the end of the day, it would have caused issues for the families if I declined the invite.

So here I am.

Dancing with the man that I have had a crush on since before I can even remember.

My body is pressed right up against his chest, and I can feel how solid his build is.

I've always wanted to know how he felt.

I giggle like a schoolgirl because that's how he makes me feel.

I let my fingers slip up his neck, into his hair and I feel the goosebumps that spread over his skin. Mm. He likes it.

"Stop that." He growls at me. Always so grumpy.

"Why are you scared of having a little fun?" I tease him.

He reaches back and drags my hand onto his shoulder.

I think maybe I just need to get him to have a few more drinks. The bridal party has been throwing back shots all night. My head is buzzing warm and fuzzy because of it.

Maybe if I get Frankie to give Mas a few extra shots, he'll relax a little.

The music changes and Mas lets out a deep sigh of regret. It's a slow song, intimate. Seductive. I rest my cheek on his chest and sway my body up against his.

Mas' massive hand is resting on my lower back and the bolts of lightning its sending through my body are delightful.

I arch my back against his hand, and he clears his throat. He can feel the way I'm moving. He's struggling with it. I can tell by the way he's trying to move away from me.

I giggle, continuing my games until the song ends and he runs off the floor, back to our table.

I follow him, and when I get there, I enthusiastically demand "Shooters." And Isabelle grins at me, lifting her empty shot glass while Frankie stands up to pour a few.

"I think Mas needs a double." I say to Frankie. He chuckles and nods.

Mas doesn't even notice when he gets handed a larger shot glass than everyone else.

Isabelle waves me over and I sit down next to her while the guys all talk on the other side of the table. I watch Frankie pouring them another shot.

"You like him, don't you?" Isabelle asks.

I nod. "You know I've had a crush on him forever."

"I know you used to - I didn't know you still did."

I roll my eyes. "Look at the guy. He's like a work of art. A sculpture."

"But he's so moody." She laughs.

"He's not moody. He's mysterious." I reply with a giggle.

"You know your father would kill you - and him."

"What my father doesn't know can't hurt him."

She nods. "Ok, well, you had better make this happen tonight then, hey?"

"I'm trying." I snap in frustration.

No matter how much I flirt with the guy, he just isn't flirting back.

To make it weirder - he keeps checking me out. I can see he enjoys looking at me, and when we dance together, I notice how tense he gets.

I'm going to make a move.

He thinks I'm pretty and he can't hide it, so I'll make a move.

He's probably just nervous about my father. That's probably all that's stopping him.

When all of us head over to the dance floor again, Mas is looking more relaxed. Frankie has made sure he's had enough shots of tequila to relax his shoulders and put a bit of a smile on his face.

I step close to him again, but this time my stomach is fluttering with a hundred butterflies. I am so nervous I can barely see straight.

I can't believe I'm going to do this.

If I kiss him - and he kisses me back - I will be the happiest girl in the entire world.

He wouldn't kiss me if he didn't have a crush on me, too.

Wrapping my arms around his neck and pressing my breasts against his solid chest, I stare up at him.

"You are relentless." He says, his deep voice vibrating against me.

His eyes are locked with mine, and I can feel the tension between us growing.

I trace my fingers over his jaw line, and he doesn't stop me. In fact, he's still looking down at me.

My eyes fall to his lips.

I feel my own lips parting.

My heart is beating faster and faster by the second.

I'm going to do it.

I'm going to kiss him.

But before I have a chance to make my move, *he leans down to kiss me.*

I can't believe it.

I'm so shocked that for a second, I forget to kiss him back.

But as his lips move against mine, the rest of the world and all of my thoughts fall silent.

I'm in heaven.

His mouth is locked over mine as he pushes his tongue between my lips.

I wrap my hand around the back of his neck and press harder against him.

I feel my entire body become alive as I rock myself against him.

A low growl rumbles through him as his hand presses hard against my lower back.

Oh, my word.

This is the most incredible thing I've ever experienced in my entire life.

The music changes and it breaks the trance I'm in.

Mas pulls his lips away from mine.

"I need another drink." He says, stepping back, his arms releasing me.

I feel lost for a second. A little bewildered.

Then Isabelle catches my eye and scrunches her nose as the biggest grins spreads across her face. My eyes are wide with excitement.

I just kissed Masaccio Vece. Literally the hottest guy on the planet.

And he kissed me back.

CHAPTER THREE
Masaccio

We are back on the dance floor, which is the last place I want to be because her tight little body is getting harder and harder to ignore when she presses it right up against me like this.

She is staring up at me. The thin strap of her dress slips a little and falls from her shoulder. Instinctively, I run my hand up her arm, dragging the strap back into place.

Her lips curve into a temptress's smile.

Her eyes are locked with mine and I can feel I am about to make a terrible decision as the alcohol blurs my self-control.

Fuck, she is gorgeous.

As she presses against me, her breasts spill from the top of her dress.

Fuck.

This is not helping.

Her lips part and her fingers trace along my jaw, sending shivers running through my body.

My cock is stirring, wanting to know what she feels like.

My eyes trace over her full, rose-pink lips. The lipstick has long faded, but her natural color is even more beautiful. I lick my lips. I wonder what she tastes like.

Not thinking clearly, I lean down - and press my mouth against hers as my hand touches the heat of her skin.

She seems to hesitate for a moment, but then melts against me. Her body rubbing against mine.

Fuck. She feels so good in my arms.

The kiss deepens as she pulls me even closer.

Her lips are soft and warm.

Sparks seem to shoot from my fingers where my hand touches her lower back.

She pushes her hips against me, and I feel my cock beginning to grow.

Shit. This isn't good. I can't let her feel that. She's already throwing herself at me. If she knows I'm physically attracted to her, there will be no end to this disaster of a situation.

I shouldn't even be kissing her.

It was impulsive. A terrible decision.

If I don't stop now, I'm going to have a problem that will not be easy to hide.

The music changes and it's enough of a distraction for me to pull away from her.

But my cock is still not ready to calm down and my heart is hammering against my ribcage. I am sure she feels it against her breasts.

I have to get out of here. I have to get away from her.

"I need a drink." I mutter and let her go, hurrying to leave.

I walk straight to the bar and order a whisky on a rocks. Dammit. That was so stupid of me. Leora Alesso is nothing but trouble, and I can't be mixing with someone like her.

I run my hands through my hair. Then I shake my head, closing my eyes and wishing I hadn't been so stupid.

"You're playing with fire." My brother says with a chuckle as he leans against the bar next to me. Rufino looks like a red-haired Viking. He's one of the very few people I've ever known who is taller than me. His presence demands attention. Most people are terrified of him.

It didn't stop me and my other brothers from ripping him off though - just for looking different.

"What?" I say, feeling moody again, eager for this wedding to be over so I can go home, have a hot shower and forget any of this happened.

"Leora. You're asking for trouble with that girl. Next, she'll be wanting a proposal and she'll be choosing names for your kids. That's not the girl you want to mess around with."

"Fuck off. She's just tipsy." I snarl, feeling more agitated by the minute. I wish he hadn't seen that. I'll never hear the end of it.

Rufino shakes his head. "She's a firecracker, that one. But I don't think she kissed you because she's tipsy. I think she's got the hots for you." He's leaning with his elbow on the bar, looking out over the crowd of guests. No doubt eyeing Leora.

My youngest brother arrives at the bar too. "Did you just kiss Leora Alesso?" He laughs, punching my arm.

"Don't you start as well."

"You guys are going to live happily ever after and tell your kids how you met at a wedding. Pretty romantic, Mas." Celso says, grinning at Rufino as he taunts me.

"What the fuck is wrong with you two?" I grumble, nodding a thanks to the barman as he slides my whisky towards me. "It was just a kiss. A drunk mistake. It didn't mean a fucking thing."

I glance over to where Leora is talking to some of her friends and immediately regret it. The looks she throws at me make my stomach knot.

I drag my eyes away.

She does look like she's ready to name our kids. Freaking hell. I need to stay clear of her.

"I heard her father has hit some trouble with his business." Rufino and Celso are chatting among themselves.

"What kind of trouble?" I ask, wanting a distraction from my bad choices. I make a point of keeping my back to the guests - to Leora. Making no accidental eye contact with her.

"I don't think his business has been bringing in any profits for a while now. He took out some loans to invest, but from what people are saying, he just ended up in debt."

"You can't trust what people say these days." I shake my head. I never was one for gossip.

"Not just any people. Even dad was commenting on it the other day. Marco Alesso is in the shit. Dad was discussing the fact that it provides an opportunity for us to move in and take over some of his territory." Rufino says.

Getting our hands on Marco's territory would be a bonus. We don't need it. But it would be nice. For my father, it would be more of an ego thing than a business thing. Marco and him have been at each other's throats for years.

"Dad has been after his territory for over a decade now." Celso takes a sip of his beer.

"I guess now's the time, then."

I stare back towards Leora. "I wonder if daddy's little princess over there knows her father isn't so rich anymore. She wouldn't survive a day in the life of a working person." I smirk.

"There are a hundred men who grab the chance to marry that fox. She's too beautiful to worry about not being a pampered princess."

"Hmph." I snort in annoyance. I don't like spoilt brats, and she is the queen of brats.

"She might be beautiful - but I pity any man who ends up having to marry that one."

Eventually, the conversation drifts away from Marco Alesso and his spoilt daughter, to far more interesting topics, like our own family business, which has been thriving.

For the rest of the wedding, I do my best to avoid Leora, not wanting to be tempted to repeat the same mistake. I hang out with my brothers and drink beers at the bar until the guest start leaving and the crowd thins out and I think I can leave too without being rude about it.

I walk over to the table where I left my jacket over the back of the chair. Picking it up, I slip my arms into the sleeves and shrug in onto my shoulders.

I feel a hand run down my back, sending a shiver through my body.

"Are you leaving already?"

I turn to face Leora.

My jaw muscles clench and my mouth is dry.

She steps close to me and runs her hand down my chest.

I catch her wrist and stop her.

"Leora, I hope you enjoy the rest of the evening." I say, stepping away from her.

"But - don't you want to get my number?" She looks hopeful.

"No, thank you." I take another step back and she steps with me, so I reach out and grab her shoulder, forcing her to stop.

"Good *night*, Leora." I say - to the point - leaving no room for misunderstanding.

She nods, a slight, tipsy grin on her face.

"Good night, Mas. I'm sure we will see each other again soon."

I turn around, walking away briskly. "I doubt it." I mutter to myself.

I hope my brothers didn't see all of that, otherwise they'll be ripping me off again.

CHAPTER FOUR
Leora

I wake up with a smile on my face. I feel as though the world is full of possibilities right now and they are all in my favor.

Rolling over, I bury my face against my pillow, giggling to myself.

I'm still high on all the emotions left over from that kiss. Wow! That kiss.

I can't believe my first kiss ever was with the hottest man on the planet, Masaccio Vece.

Rolling onto my back, I stretch my legs out, yawn, and assess my body. I don't have a hangover - which is pretty impressive considering how many shots we had last night.

Wow. That was so much fun. That was the best wedding I have ever been to.

And I kissed Masaccio Vece - *and he kissed me back*.

That means he likes me.

I wonder why he didn't want to take my phone number.

Maybe he was just being cautious. It's the right thing to do. Maybe I should be cautious too. I can't just go around messaging him whenever I feel like it - I have a sneaky feeling dad is tracking my phone. It wouldn't surprise me, considering how controlling he is.

Taking a deep breath in and letting it out with a happy, dreamy smile on my face, I throw the blankets off me and hop out of bed.

Oh, my word.

I am so in love with that man.

We kissed.

I want to tell everyone. But that would be a terrible idea.

I can't wait to see him again. Even if we have to date in secret. It will be worth it. I would do anything for him. He's my dream man.

I skip down the stairs and into the kitchen to make a coffee.

It's a bit later than I expected it to be. I guess I slept off what would have been the hangover, so I can't complain about that.

"Daddy?" I call out into the house while I'm making my coffee. But there is no reply.

He must be in the West wing, or maybe out somewhere already.

I press the button on the coffee machine, and it shoots rich dark coffee into my mug, followed by a creamy froth of milk.

I love starting my day with a cup of coffee, but it has to be made right.

Daddy doesn't drink coffee, but he got this coffee machine for me anyway and I went on a fun little barista course to learn how to use it. So did the house staff - just in case I ask one of them to make me a coffee.

I carry my mug out onto the patio, blinking against the warm morning sunlight. It feels brighter than usual. Maybe I do have a teeny tiny hangover.

I don't care though. I'm so happy.

"Poppet. You're awake. Good. I need to talk to you."

My father steps through the patio doors and walks towards me.

"Morning daddy. Did you have a nice evening last night?" I ask.

"Mm. Not really. I spent it with the family accountant, going over the financial records." He says in a stressed tone.

"Is that bad?" I ask, feeling a little anxious because of his demeanor. I put my coffee down on the nearby table and turn my attention towards him.

He's going to tell me I can't get that new Lexus I've had my eye on. He always starts these dramatic sounding conversations about money - and then tells me I can't have something I want.

"Listen, Poppet." He clears his throat and swallows hard as though his mouth is dry. Then he sits down on the outside sofa and pulls me down to sit next to him. "Leora, I lost a large portion of my territory last week. I was trying to save it, but I couldn't. It's gone. The whole stretch along the docks. Right by the shipping yards. Valuable land. It went to a rival family. Now I am about to lose my two warehouses on the other side of the docks and if that happens, I won't have any space that allows me to ship products out—" I'm not sure what to say.

He sighs and presses his fingers into his eyes as though he has a headache.

"I'm sure you can fix it daddy. You always fix things." I say.

I reach out and touch his knee, trying to comfort him.

"No, not this time. This time I had to make some tough decisions. And it's a decision that involves you."

I sit up a little straighter, feeling tensed by his words. "Me?"

"Poppet, I need to keep my place at the table. If I don't - we will lose everything. The house, the cars, everything. I had to—"

"What is going on daddy?" I blurt out, not able to take the suspense anymore. I wish he would just tell me instead of dragging it out like this.

"Leora, I've had to agree to an arranged marriage. The marriage will be between you and one of our rival families."

"Who?" I shout in horror. "You can't do this." My heart is pulling and pushing at the same time, and I feel nausea building in my stomach.

"I have a meeting this afternoon with the family - it will be finalized by the end of the day. I'm sorry poppet but I had no choice."

I stand up, fuming at how ridiculous this is. He can't force me to marry someone. I'm in love with Mas. Him and I are meant to be together. He kissed me last night.

"You can't do this daddy. I won't marry whoever you're making this arrangement with. I want to get married for love." I sound like a complete brat, throwing a tantrum. But trust me - you would too if you were just giving the same news.

"Sit down poppet, please."

"Who is it?" I demand, with my arms folded across my chest as I glare down at my father.

"I am meeting with Vincent Vece. It will be one of his sons." My father's voice is filled with regret.

I stare at him in disbelief. Did I hear that right?

Vincent Vece.

Masaccio's father.

"Are you serious?" I blurt out.

My father's guilty expression morphs into a frown. "Yes." He says, watching my expression.

Shit.

I'm forgetting that the Vece's are our enemies - regardless of what is happening between Mas and me.

"Daddy, you have to do what you have to do for the family." I say, sitting down at taking his hands in mine. "I understand and I won't make this more difficult than it has to be."

My father chews at the inside of his cheek, watching me.

I pout a little. Trying to look at least a little upset about this whole thing.

I mean, Mas is not the only single brother. It could be any of them.

This doesn't automatically mean I am going to end up marrying him. All of his brothers are super-hot though - but he's the one I want. I think that as soon as he finds out about the arrangement between our fathers, he will jump at the opportunity to marry me.

I purse my lips to hide the smile touching my face.

"I'm going to go shower." I stand up, needing to get away from my dad. "What time is your meeting? When will you know?"

"I'll be home at five this evening and we can talk about what was arranged over dinner tonight. I'm really sorry about this poppet. You know - if there was any other way - I would have taken it."

I reach out and squeeze his shoulder. "Daddy, it's going to be ok. It won't be so bad. Whatever keeps our family safe is all that matters to me."

He pulls me into a hug.

"Thank you, Poppet." He says, sounding relieved.

I rush upstairs, taking the steps two at a time.

I can just feel it in my heart. The universe is giving me the most beautiful gift. Mas and I are going to get married. It's destiny. He *must* be my soulmate. It all started aligning last night when we danced together - the kiss just sealed our fate - and from that moment on there was nothing in the universe that could keep us apart - not even the fact that our fathers are enemies.

CHAPTER FIVE
Masaccio

"Why are we having a meeting with Marco Alesso, anyway?" I ask, following my father into his office. He is planning to retire soon - then this will become my office.

Ever since I was little, before I even understood the concept of business, my father has been training me to take over from him.

I am the oldest son. The first born.

Even my identical twin brother, Tuomo, won't be consider an heir because he was born a full three minutes after me.

"Mas just leave the questions for later. I have a lot of my mind right now."

"You want me to join you at the meeting having no idea what it is about?"

"You'll be fine. You always handle yourself well in business situations."

"So, it is business related?"

"Of course." My father nods, but he isn't looking at me, his attention is on the paperwork on his desk.

It's for the best that he isn't looking at me, anyway. He reads me too well. He would notice the relief in my expression. The meeting is business related. That means it has nothing to do with the fact that I kissed Leora Alesso.

The thought of her father finding out and the drama that would cause - I just don't have the patience or the energy to deal with that kind of nonsense.

I wonder what it is my father wants with him then.

Our family is much stronger than his - and if the rumors are true and Marco is struggling financially perhaps, he wants to grovel a little and ask my father for money.

That would be like throwing fire on my father's ego. He would love to watch Marco groveling. He would love to be able to make Marco suffer in any way at all.

Fuck.

This meeting is going to be a bunch of old men bullshit and a bunch of politics. I guess that's what most business is.

Soon I will take over from my father and makes some much-needed changes to this business. It needs some life injected into its veins. Something new, young, fresh.

My father still does things old school. It works. But there is room for improvement that he is not yet interested in hearing about.

"What time is the meeting? I want to grab a coffee?"

"No time. Marco will be here in a minute or two."

Just as my father replies one of his men comes through to knock on the office door.

"Sir, he's here."

"Good, send him to the board room. We'll be right up."

My father takes his time finishing what he is busy with. It's a power play - making Marco wait.

I say nothing.

When my father stands and pulls his jacket on, I ask, "you sure you don't want to give me a heads up regarding what this is about?"

"No. Come on."

Marco stands when we walk into the board room and my father diplomatically accepts his hand to shake it.

"You've met my oldest son, Masaccio. He will be taking over the family business one day."

"Good to meet you, Masaccio." Marco says. His voice is tight. His shoulders are so tense they look knotted and stiff. His jaw muscles are clenched. When he sits down again, he is sitting as though there is a metal rod shoved into his spine. Perfectly straight.

Whatever the reason for him being here - he's not comfortable or happy about it. I'd place bets on how difficult this is for him. It must be true. His business must be suffering. I guess he's here to ask for a loan of sorts.

I take a seat, sitting comfortably at the table. Waiting for the two old men to talk.

"So, Marco. You told me what you wanted over the phone, why don't you start from the beginning and tell me in more detail." My father says a smug grin on his face. He's loving this.

Marco clears his throat. "Vincent. You know by now that I lost the stretch of territory next to the docks - and I am about to lose the two warehouses on the other side. It is my only entry point for getting my shipments out and if I lose that territory I lose my place at the table, I lose everything." He pulls his mouth tight. He's really struggling. The truth is even worse than the rumors. His business is scraps at this point.

"Alright. And what did you want to do?" my father asks, leaning back in his chair and folding his arms across his chest.

"I want to make a deal with you. I will give you what we discussed, and you will cover the debt I owe in order for me to keep my warehouses."

He takes a heavy breath, holding it in for a long time before blowing it out.

My father is taking his time giving his answer. I know he already has one. He's just playing games at this point. He's making the moment last because he's enjoying himself.

"So, you are still going ahead with what we discussed on the phone?"

"Yes, my daughter, Leora."

At the mention of her name my ears prickle and my attention turns towards Marco.

"Leora?" Her name is out of my mouth before I have a chance to stop myself, but I was not expecting him to talk about her today.

"Yes, Leora has agreed as well. She will not give you any trouble. Have you decided which of your sons she will marry?" Marco asks and my heart leaps into my throat as realization slams into me.

What the fuck?

An arranged marriage. That is what this meeting is about?

I clench my teeth together to stop myself from reacting emotionally.

"Masaccio will marry Leora." My father says the words, but my brain denies them.

I feel myself staring at him, but I don't seem to see anything except white smudges that blur my vision.

"Masaccio? Oh, that's good. Your oldest." Marco says.

"You want me to marry her?" I blurt out, aiming the question at my father.

"Yes, Masaccio. You spend far too much time working, and this is an excellent opportunity for you to get a wife."

"Rufino and Celso are also unmarried and would be better suited." I argue.

Marco has gone silent as the back and forth between my father and I grow tense.

My father shoots me a warning look. "Masaccio, you are to marry the girl. It has already been decided."

Now is not the time to fight this. Not in front of Marco.

But my father knew what he was doing by not letting me know what this meeting was about.

"Marco, I will arrange everything. Once the wedding is concluded, our families will have entered an alliance. Your warehouses will remain safe and in your name." My father confirms, ending the meeting.

I don't utter another word until Marco leaves. I don't even say goodbye to the man.

Then I turn towards my father, fuming with rage. My fists clenched at my side.

"What the hell was that. You blindsided me and you know it." I snap.

He doesn't even flinch. He was expecting this - which makes me even more angry about it.

"Masaccio, you have to marry one day. May as well be now."

"No, not that girl. Get Celso to marry her. Tuomo, Rufino - any of them - I really don't care. Just not me. I have too much to do. I don't have time to get married and deal with that shit."

My father turns towards me with his brows knotted and his eyes narrowed. His gaze is sharp and pierces into me.

"You *are* going to marry that girl. It is my decision, and you will do it. I know that if you don't end up in an arranged marriage, you'll never get married. This is the way it's happening. She's a beautiful girl. I don't understand what your problem is."

"I'll get married one day - I will - just not to her."

"Bullshit. When last did you even go on a date or look at a woman with interest? You bury yourself in work. You hardly socialize. No. This is done. It's decided. You are marrying her, and I won't hear another word."

I grit my teeth. I know the limits of when I can and can't disagree with my father's decisions and he won't tolerate me talking back again. He let me have my say - and now it's done.

I am going to have to marry that fucking girl. The one girl on the planet that I would never ever want to marry.

CHAPTER SIX
Leora

There are people all around me, rushing back and forth in a noisy, beautiful chaotic and energetic buzz. I am so excited I want to scream.

It's my wedding day.

I'm marrying the first man I ever kissed. My first crush.

I can't believe it.

I'm the luckiest girl in the world.

When my father came home that night, after his meeting with Vincent Vece - when he told me I was going to be marrying the oldest son, Masaccio - I almost cried I was so happy. I really struggled to hide my emotions. I didn't want my dad to know I even knew Masaccio because it might have upset him.

But today is different. I don't care at this point if my dad finds out I knew Mas before the arrangements were made - it's too late to change anything.

I don't have to hide how I feel because today is going to be the happiest day of my life, and I want to celebrate every single moment of it.

"Here, stand still, wait, let me clip it in." Isabelle grabs my arms and turns me to face the mirror. "Will you calm down? It's like you've had too much caffeine or something." She complains, trying to clip the tiara into the braided curls on top of my head. I am wiggling and dancing on the spot. I have too much energy to stand still.

"Put it further forward, the veil is going there." I point to the back of my head.

"Oh, right?" She pins it into my hair and then rests her chin on my shoulder from behind me. "You really look *so* beautiful. I can't believe it was *my* wedding just the other day - and now it's yours - I never - in a million years - could have seen this coming." She laughs.

"I think I always knew. Somehow. I've always felt there was something special between Mas and me." I haven't admitted that to anyone out loud. It feels good to say it. It feels real and true.

She shakes her head, still smiling. "Alright. Let's get all the bridesmaids together and do a final make up check and then I think we are ready to get going."

Isabelle turns away from me and calls the bridesmaids together.

Dalila, Masaccio's sister, is my maid of honor. She seems just as excited as I am about her older brother getting married.

"Are we ready?" She asks Isabelle as she comes to stand with us. "Oh, my word, Leora, you look so beautiful."

"Thanks." I grin. I look beautiful. I feel like a princess.

I don't know why but Masaccio's father has gone overboard with everything. I saw the cake this morning. It's the size of a car. And the decorations had my jaw on the floor. The venue is massive, I don't even know how many people are coming, but every wall, every corner, every table is dripping with white and cream flowers. Chandeliers are hanging over every table too, and the lighting - oh my word it is to die for. I couldn't even have dreamed up a more amazing setting. I think he hired the best of the best when it came to decorators and planners.

"Ladies, they are ready for you—" The wedding planner sticks her head through the doorway and starts ushering us out into the hall.

My stomach flips with nervous excitement.

I am about to marry the man of my dreams.

Someone hands me a bunch of flowers. Roses and lilies and giant cream daffodils. They smell lovely.

As I'm walking, Dalila rushes over to me and clips the veil into my hair. "I can't believe we almost forgot that." She laughs, then walks next to me towards the church.

My mind falls silent when the church organ plays and beautiful music seeps into my heart. The church doors open, and I walk towards them - my feet don't feel like they belong to me. I feel like I'm in a movie.

I gasp when I see him standing at the altar.

He is wearing a crisp black tuxedo. A single white rose tucked into the pocket. His face is stern, serious, his eyes piercing into me.

A massive smile stretches across my cheeks, and I am sure he can see how happy I am. I want him to know how happy I am.

We haven't even seen each other since the night we kissed.

I haven't said a word to him since then.

And now I am about to marry him.

I walk past my friends and family, glancing towards my father with a broad smile. He isn't smiling. I know this is hard for him. If only I could be really honest about how I've dreamed of this moment since I first saw Masaccio.

Then my attention is on him. My soon to be husband.

The priest talks for a long time, and I hear him in the distance, behind my thoughts of how gorgeous Mas looks. He is just staring at me. Not smiling, not moving. He's taking this very seriously.

"I now pronounce you man and wife. You may kiss your bride."

This is the moment I have been waiting for. I take a breath, waiting for him to step forward and sweep me backwards like they do in the movies.

He steps forward. His hand touches my hip. He gently, quickly kisses my lips.

What the fuck was that?

Confusion seeps into me.

Was that it?

Was that our magical moment wedding kiss?

He takes my hand and pulls me down the aisle to walk towards the doors.

Maybe he's shy, it might embarrass him to kiss me in front of all of these people.

The kiss we shared on the dance floor was a hundred times more intense than that one.

It's ok. We have our whole lives ahead of us now and plenty of beautiful moments together.

At the reception hundreds of people are congratulating us. Most of them I don't know, but I'm so happy I just enjoy every second.

Masaccio gets called aside by one of his brothers and my father comes to stand with me.

He looks sour.

"Daddy, aren't you having fun? This wedding is just—"

"It's over the top. It's way over the top. He did this on purpose." He whispers in a harsh tone.

"What do you mean? Who did what on purpose?" I ask confused.

"Vincent Vece. He spent more money on this wedding that what he is giving me to clear my debt. And he invited the entire planet just so that he could rub it in my face." He snaps.

I bite my lip. I wish my father didn't see it that way. I am having the most incredible time.

"Daddy, it's a beautiful wedding. It's *my* wedding. Your daughter is only going to get married once - so please try to enjoy it."

"Hmph." He huffs, still angry, not letting go of his bitterness over this whole thing.

Masaccio returns to my side.

"Masaccio. Congratulations. I am sure you two will be very happy together." My father says through tight lips.

"Thank you. I am sure we will." Masaccio replies, just as tense and tight-lipped.

I roll my eyes. Are all the men in my life sulking on my most beautiful wedding day.

I slip my arm through Mas's and grin up at him.

"Are you ready for our first dance as husband and wife?" I ask, deciding to ignore all the dark moodiness between the men.

Mas nods.

"Good." I wave at Isabelle, and she comes hurrying over.

"You can tell them we are ready for our first dance." My heart spins.

The lights are dimmed low and there is a soft spotlight on us. Fairy lights are glittering above us and the music is drifting through the air. I am pressed right against him, feeling warm, safe and happy.

My husband.

The man I kissed and started to fall in love with.

I can't wait to spend every day with him for the rest of my life.

I smile as we move together, letting the music guide us.

He feels a little stiff, perhaps tense because there are so many people watching us.

I can't wait to get home - our first night alone together - and the magical things that are going to happen.

It is, after all, our wedding night.

CHAPTER SEVEN
Masaccio

The entire wedding is hell.

I am tired of smiling and playing the part of a happy husband. In all honesty, I have been doing a pretty shit job of even pretending to be happy.

My father sat me down an hour before the wedding started and gave me one hell of a lecture on putting on a show for the guests and the media who are flocking this event like flies on shit.

The constant bombardment of *congratulations*, and *I wish you two all the happiness*, and *wow you look so in love* - I can't take it anymore. I want this night to be over so that I can go home, take off this fucking tuxedo and sleep.

Maybe when I wake up in the morning, this will all be a bad dream.

Of course, no matter how much I pretend it's all a nightmare - I know Leora is coming home with me. My home is now her home.

My father arranged for her things to be brought over earlier this week and now she is going to be living with me from tonight.

Fuck sakes.

What the hell is happening to my life?

All night I have been keeping her at a polite distance to try not to give her the wrong idea.

It's clear she is thrilled by all of this. She's having the time of her life.

I've been watching her all night, and she hasn't stopped smiling once.

Every chance she gets she clings on to me, holding me, wrapping her arms around me, holding my hand -

I am going to have to be stricter about all of this in order to make it even more clear after tonight.

This whole thing is just for show.

She needs to understand that.

There is no love here and there never will be.

That mistake I made the other night kissing her - it's haunting me even more now that we are married.

Fuck. Married. I can't believe it.

Our first dance ends and with relief I step away from her as other guests flood the dance floor.

She tries to pull me back towards her and I shake my head.

"I'm done dancing, Leora." I say. Her eyes soften a little, a small amount of the sparkle leaves them.

I know she isn't happy about me putting boundaries up - but she needs to learn the reality of us being married.

It's still early for a party and some guests are only just feeling the vibe of the champagne now. I will not stay much longer though.

Besides, even just for show, they would expect a newlywed couple to want to rush off home. It won't be weird if I grab my wife and leave my own celebration.

With that thought I smile. Now is as good a time as any. We've done all the things required for a traditional ceremony. We've danced, cut the cake, listened to the speeches, thrown the garter - yes - I can leave now.

I walk straight towards Nathan. My right-hand man.

"Have the driver bring the car around front. I'm ready to leave."

"Yes, sir."

"And bring my wife. She can meet me in the car."

I don't even have the patience to wait and walk out with her at this point. I've used up every bit of my will power on pretenses this evening.

I grab my tuxedo jacket off the back of my chair at the bride and groom's table. Tossing it over my shoulder and I walk straight out of the venue without looking back and without making eye contact with a single person because I am not in the mood to get roped into one more conversation about what it feels like to be a married man now.

The driver is already there when I step outside into the cool night air.

I climb in and wait for Leora. Nathan won't take long bringing her out.

I glance towards the venue doors just in time to see him leading her through them, towards the car. She looks confused.

He pulls the limo door open, and half pushes her inside.

"Masaccio? What is going on?"

"I'm done here, it's time to go home."

"Oh." She says with surprise. "I didn't say bye to anyone."

"They'll be fine. Come on, let him close the door - lets go home."

She grins at me and shifts across the seat to be close to me, bunching the layers of her wedding dress around her legs to get comfortable.

"Home." She says, smiling.

I turn my face to look out of the other window, away from her, and ignore the way she is resting her head on my shoulder.

Should I say something? Should I tell her to move?

Best to ignore it. It's been a long night. I can talk to her tomorrow about what will and won't be happening in our relationship.

When the car arrives at my house I climb out, hardly even waiting for it to come to a stop - and not opening her door for her. The driver can deal with that.

I head straight inside and to my room, stripping out of the tuxedo and tossing it to the floor.

Thank fuck that's over.

I climb into the shower and push it all the way to the hot side, letting the water scald over my skin, burning away the agitation I have been feeling all day.

When I climb out of the shower and head back into my room with the towel wrapped around my waist all the relaxation that the shower provided disappears in an instant.

She's standing at the foot of my bed - in white lingerie.

Fuck she looks sexy.

I grit my teeth. I do not want to do this and give her the wrong impression.

She walks slowly towards me.

"Hi, husband." She says, reaching out and running her fingers down my chest.

Her breasts wrapped in white lace, the garter belt holding up thigh-high stockings.

My eyes roam over her tight figure, perfect curves - dammit.

No.

I can't do this.

My cock has other ideas though as it throbs.

She presses herself against me, standing on her tiptoes as she lifts her face towards mine.

I look down at her, my eyes on her lips, I could just -

"I've been waiting for this night my whole life. The night I get to give myself to my husband." She whispers.

What the fuck?

"You've never—are you a—" I stammer in shock.

She nods, smiling the naughtiest and cutest smile.

"I am. I wanted my wedding night to be really special."

My cock is getting harder by the second. A virgin.

This is not good.

I place both hands on her shoulders and firmly push her away.

Not a fucking chance am I doing that.

If I sleep with her, now she will read too much into it. It's not worth it.

Sure, she's hot. She's fucking hot. But I will not take her virginity on our wedding night and have her thinking its love.

"This isn't happening. You need to leave." I say as I push her away from me.

"Leave? I —"

"Yes, go to your own room." I snap.

"I'm not sleeping in your room? But - we're married?" her eyes are wide with confusion. The corners of her mouth turned down. She stands looking awkwardly out of place, lifting her arm to cover her chest in a self-conscious gesture.

"Yes, Leora. This wedding was for show. Now go to your own room. I don't know why you even came in here in the first place."

I can feel the harshness of my words as they spill from my mouth, but I know I have to make this clear - right from the start. I wasn't going to do it tonight, but apparently, I have no choice.

She expects far too much from me.

If it was just sex - nothing else - I'd be there in a heartbeat. But she wants more than that. And I will not give it to her.

Leora stares at me for a moment, then nods, turns away and hurries out of the room, to her own room across the hall.

I breathe a sigh of relief.

Climbing into my bed I pull the covers up over my shoulders and close my eyes.

I can hear her now. The soft, muffled sounds of her crying.

Fuck.

I think I was too harsh.

She was excited - I mean - it's her wedding night.

I roll over and try to ignore her tears, but the sounds continue to drift through my open door.

I could get up and close it, but she would hear that, and it might hurt her even more.

I am an asshole.

I know I am.

It's better that she learns that now rather than later.

I pick up the other pillow and press it over my ears, doing my best to block out her crying - and my guilt.

CHAPTER EIGHT
Leora

My wedding night was one of the worst nights of my life. The rejection hit me so hard. And I still don't understand it. It still hurts to think about it. Mas was so cold and abrupt. He pushed me away and didn't even want to sleep in the same room as me.

I thought he wanted to marry me. I'm so confused.

And I know men have needs - isn't it normal to sleep with your spouse.

We are married. Married couples have sex.

Maybe he's not attracted to me?

No - that can't be right. I think I'm pretty. He seemed into me when he kissed me - so why in the world did he turn me down on our wedding night?

I know if he just lets go of whatever he has against intimacy then we can get to know each other more and we can build an actual relationship.

We have just landed in Hawaii, and I am over the moon with excitement as we step off the private jet.

He has been his usual quiet self the entire flight, but now that we're here, the vibe is going to bring him out of his shell. I just know it.

People rush towards us, throwing strings of beautiful flowers around our necks. Bright red and yellow. Our car is already waiting here for us and the driver is busy loading our luggage while Masaccio and I stand listening to the welcoming song as Hawaiian dancers sway their hips. It's gorgeous, and so much fun.

I giggle and jump a little, grabbing Masaccio's hand. He pulls his hand back.

Asshole. I will break him down.

He'll soften over the next week.

The driver comes over to us. "Mr. And Mrs. Vece, we are ready to take you to your accommodation."

Driving through Hawaii feels like I have been transported into a different world. This is nothing like the city at home.

It's like I'm in a movie. Everything looks so perfect. Bright, warm sunshine is flooding everything, and the ocean looks so blue it's almost like someone painted it that way.

Our accommodation is a beach villa. The back step opens right up onto the beach. The white sand is right up against the house.

I can't believe this. It's a dream come true.

Masaccio doesn't look impressed at all as we walk through the villa. He picks up an apple from the fruit basket and eats it, glancing around as though he's seen this all a hundred times.

"This place is magical." I say, skipping around the sofa to open the big glass sliding doors.

"Mm. Yeah. It's great." Mas says with zero enthusiasm.

"Do you think we can go diving while we're here? I've always wanted to try that."

"You can go diving. Do whatever you want." He turns his back on me and walks out of the living room area towards the kitchen.

I follow him, a playfulness in my step. "Are you hungry? Shall we go out for some seafood?"

"No. I'm going to make a toasted cheese and then get some sleep." He replies blandly.

"Mm. Ok."

If he wants to lie down for a while I have the perfect idea.

Up in the bedroom I pull my suitcase open and start searching for my black silk nightie. The white didn't seem to catch his attention enough, so I'll try black this time.

It's our first night on our honeymoon - all the pressure from the wedding is over - so I think he will be much more relaxed - and enthusiastic.

I giggle as I head into the bathroom to change.

Wrapping a long silk gown, also black, around myself to hide what I'm wearing - I want to keep it a surprise. I wait, listening for him - he won't be long.

But it feels like ages has passed and I hear nothing.

I sigh, getting bored with all the waiting.

Finally, when I think he must have changed his mind about having a sleep after lunch - I head downstairs to find him.

And he's asleep on the sofa.

He fell asleep down here.

I giggle. Poor guy was so tired he didn't even make it up stairs. No wonder he seemed so disinterested in the villa.

I push him a little, shifting him over so that I can lie down next to him. In his sleep he mumbles but moves easily enough.

I drop the gown to the floor, feeling the smooth fabric as it brushes over my skin, then I lie down next to him, pulling his arm and wrapping it around my waist.

I snuggle with my back against his chest, pressing my ass against his cock.

I close my eyes, a grin on my face, knowing he won't be able to resist the feel of this silk when he wakes up.

I can't sleep, because being this close to him makes every cell of my body feel alive.

I press my ass a little harder against his cock and he stirs slightly. His arm tightens around my waist, pulling me closer to him.

I gasp.

My heart beats a million miles an hour.

I hear him mumble something I can't make out. He's talking in his sleep.

His hand travels over my waist and I feel him thrusting his hips forward a little.

His cock is growing harder.

I move my hips in small circles. Feeling so turned on at his touch.

"Leora?" he says in shock, shifting his hips away from me so that I can no longer feel how hard he is. "What the fuck?" he mutters.

He sits up, half pushing me off the sofa. "What are you doing?"

"You said you wanted to sleep for a little while after lunch, so I was lying with you." I say innocently. "But seeing as you're awake now maybe—" I sit up and turn to face him, sitting on my knees with my legs spread wide. His eyes trail over my body, the skimpy black silk hardly covering anything at all.

He clears his throat, and I see how he has to force himself to look away.

"I'm going to shower." He grabs my hips, lifts me out of the way, stands up and sets me back down on the sofa. "Alone." He says.

I stare at his back as he walks away from me. Why doesn't he want me?

Biting my lip, I look down at what I'm wearing. It's cute. It's better than cute - it's really sexy.

I sigh and flop back against the sofa.

You know what - it's just a challenge that's all.

I'll embrace the challenge - it'll make it so much better when he is ready.

Except that the entire week of our honeymoon - no matter what I do - he rejects me.

I try the pink lace, the black lace, the red lace and even wearing nothing at all.

I try being a little forceful, and a little playful and he ignores me.

He doesn't even want to take me for dinners or lunches or join me for walks on the beach.

He's boring. Or he just finds me boring. I don't know. I don't understand at all.

It's started to get really exhausting just trying to get him to make love to me. I never expected it to be this difficult. I mean, he doesn't even want to eat breakfast with me - so how can I convince him to have sex with me?

By the second to the last day of our honeymoon, we have hardly spoken at all and I'm feeling miserable.

I'm accepting that he is just not interested in me.

I don't really want to believe that this is how my married life is going to be - but I don't know what else to do.

Maybe I need to give him a little bit of space for now and when we get home, I can try again.

He married me. I'm his wife. He's a man - doesn't he have needs for affection and connection just like everyone else in the world?

I just need to be patient - that's all.

The flight back home I am a lot more quiet than usual. I keep to myself and read a book I purchased in Hawaii. I let him be. Because that's what he seems to want for now.

Maybe, just maybe, he prefers to be the one who chases, and he doesn't like me to be so forward. So, I'll step back and wait for him to come to me this time.

CHAPTER NINE
Masaccio

I toss the file of papers across my desk. The file skids across the surface and the papers spill out onto the floor. Floating to the ground.

I'm at the office in my warehouse on the docks. I had to get out of the house. Leaning back in my chair I run my hands through my hair. My mood has been terrible lately.

My patience is gone, my frustration levels are high - I'm really struggling.

It's all because of *her*. Leora is driving me crazy.

She paraded around during our honeymoon in the sexiest, skimpiest outfits. She has been taunting me and teasing me since we got married. Her tight little body and that forward feisty attitude of her is making it harder and harder for me to say no.

But I know the moment I give in to her she will assume it's an emotional connection and that will be even more draining for me. I can't handle her. I've never lived with a woman. I've never had one spend this much time in such close proximity to me.

I don't know what to do with her.

I have to keep saying no.

But how?

I, really need her to stop looking so fucking sexy all the time.

Fuck.

I'm annoyed.

Tuomo walks into my office. He looks me up and down, frowning.

"Dude, what the hell is your problem? You look furious."

"My wife." I snap. "She won't leave me alone."

"What do you mean? Like she's nagging at you all the time or something? Complaining about things?"

"No, she wants sex. She throws herself at me. She won't stop."

"You mean—you haven't—" he looks shocked as he drags the other chair over to my desk and slumps down into it.

"Not a chance."

"But she's your *wife*. I don't get it. It's default - isn't it?"

"She's not like an *actual* wife, man. We are supposed to just live together. Our lives aren't intertwined or anything. It was forced on me. You know that."

"Ok, but you can still fuck her?"

"It's more trouble than it's worth. I don't want that from her."

He shakes his head. "I don't believe you for a second. She's hot man."

"Yeah, sure. She's gorgeous. But if I give in once she'll expect it all the time, plus other kinds of intimacy. And to make matters worse - she's a fucking virgin."

Tuomo sits dead straight in his chair.

"Your wife is a *virgin*, and she's throwing herself at you and you keep turning her down?"

I nod.

"Fuck. What I would give to be you for one night." He chuckles, looking down at his hands and then pressing his palm against his knuckles to click them.

I watch him, my thoughts bolting off in random directions.

Be me for one night.

He could. He could be me. He looks identical to me.

Maybe she's just desperate to lose her virginity and then she'll drop this whole fucking issue. Losing your virginity is kind of part of the whole marriage ceremony. It could be why she's been acting the way she has.

Maybe she just needs to be fucked - and then she'll get over it.

I clench and unclench my jaw, my brows knotting as I find myself lost in thought.

Tuomo is speaking to me - I wasn't listening.

"Hey, asshole, I'm talking to you - did you finish up with the spreadsheet—"

"Why don't you be me for one night?" I blurt out.

"Huh?" he looks blankly at me, as though I'm speaking a different language.

"Come over to my place, be me, give her what she wants, then leave."

"Funny man. Good one."

"I'm not joking." I say.

He looks up at me, his eyes piercing into mine.

"You are fucking serious. What the hell do you hope to achieve by doing this?"

"I recon - she's desperate to lose her virginity right. Like she waited, dreaming about her wedding night - blah blah blah - and now it hasn't happened. I don't think this is about me at all. I think she just wants to lose her virginity and then she might calm the fuck down."

Tuomo chuckles, shaking his head as his eyes narrow towards me. He folds his arms across his chest. "You're nuts."

"Yeah, well at this point I'm willing to try anything to get her off my back."

He leans into the chair, thinking hard. I wait, patiently.

"Alright. I'll do it." He smiles.

I stare at him for a few seconds. Wondering if this is the right choice. But like I said. I'm willing to try anything.

That night Tuomo arrives after Leora has gotten ready for bed. I can hear soft music coming from her room. I open the front door for him as quietly as I can.

He's wearing a black suit as I told him too because that's what I was wearing all day today.

My stomach knots when he walks in.

Again, I wonder if I am making the right choice, but I know I am.

She can have what she wants - and then I can get back to my life without being pestered the whole time.

Tuomo nods towards me, he doesn't say a word.

I stay downstairs as he walks up towards her bedroom.

I wait, listening, but I can't hear anything.

Curiosity gets the better of me and I make my way to the upstairs landing, standing in the hallway just outside her open door.

"Oh, Mas. Did you need something?" I hear her voice over the soft music.

I hear a shuffle and then she gasps.

"Oh." She murmurs.

I hear something get knocked over and her giggles drift out towards me.

Again, curiosity gets the better of me as I peak around the door frame, doing my best to stay out of sight, but wanting to see what's going on.

Tuomo has her lifted in his arms, her ass on the dresser, her legs wrapped around his waist. His hand is behind her neck as he kisses her with fierce passion.

Her nightie is creeping up her thighs and I can see she isn't wearing anything underneath it. A low growl rumbles through my chest.

I've made a mistake. But now it's too late to stop what's happening.

She is my wife.

I wasn't thinking when I made this choice.

I hear her giggle again and then my twin brother says something in a deep tone.

Every muscle in my body is tense.

Do I storm in there and stop this?

Will I make it worse if I do?

I should just walk away.

I should just forget about this.

"What the hell is going on?" Leora shouts angrily.

I hear something crashing and Tuomo repeating. "Hey, ok, ok, calm down."

"I will not calm down. Get out of here. You can't do this." She's horrified, but I don't know why.

I turn back towards the door, wondering why she would be so angry with 'me' for trying to sleep with her after she's been throwing herself at me for weeks.

But then she screams my name.

"Masaccio." She shouts it loudly.

"Jeez woman. Calm down. There's no need to shout, I'm right here." Tuomo says.

"How stupid do you think I am? I know you're not him. *Tuomo.*" She's angry. And it seems - she somehow knew -

"What the fuck?" He stammers.

She throws something, and it flies through the open door, missing him. "Get out." She screams.

Tuomo comes marching out of the bedroom door. His face like thunder. His shirt unbuttoned and his jacket in his hand.

"She's all yours." He snaps as he storms past, down the stairs towards the front door.

I step into her room as I hear the front door slam.

"Mas—" she says, looking terrified. "I'm so sorry. I didn't know—I thought it was you—I kissed your brother —I'm so—" Her expression is one of absolute distress. She is clutching at her nightie against her body - he took it off her.

I am both fascinated and turned on by this scene.

"How did you know it was my brother?"

"Because I know you." She whimpers. "Will you ever forgive me? I promise you I stopped as soon as I realized."

"But what was it that gave it away?" I ask curiously. I still can't drag my eyes off her as she shifts her weight from one foot to the other. The small piece of fabric that she has pressed against her chest is hardly covering anything.

CHAPTER TEN
Leora

Masaccio pushes himself between my legs, grabbing a handful of my hair he pulls my head back and traces kisses over my neck.

Sitting on the dresser with him standing in front of me, I wrap my legs around his waist.

Oh, my word.

I can't believe he has finally given in to being with me. He wants me.

He presses his lips against mine and kisses me. It's passionate, fiery, heated - but something feels - different.

Maybe it's just my own nerves.

I run my hands down his back, my nails leaving lines in his skin beneath his shirt.

"You're fucking gorgeous." He growls against my ear. "And I am going to fuck you so hard you won't be able to stand tomorrow."

I gasp at his words, but still - something feels off.

He lifts me, using his hips to push my legs wider apart and I feel how hard his cock is up against me.

I want this so badly, and I've waited so long for him to come to me, but now it just feels wrong.

He chuckles, a low sound that rumbles through me, and when I realize that even his laugh seems off - a bolt of lightning slams into me.

This isn't Masaccio.

"What the hell is going on?" I shout as I push him away.

He doesn't really budge so I kick back on the dresser and end up knocking something off it.

Tuomo lifts is hands in the air defensively "Hey, ok, ok, calm down."

"I will not calm down. Get out of here. You can't do this." I'm so angry I'm shaking. What the fuck is he doing in my room?

"Masaccio." I scream for my husband to come and help me. I need him here. Now.

"Jeez woman. Calm down. There's no need to shout, I'm right here." Tuomo says.

"How stupid do you think I am? I know you're not him. *Tuomo.*"

"What the fuck?" He stammers.

I reach behind me and grab the first thing I wrap my fingers around and throw it at him. He ducks, and it flies through the open door behind him.

He snarls at me, then grabs his jacket and spins away from me. I breathe a sigh of relief. Thank fuck. He's leaving. I want to cry. I feel disgusting.

I feel filthy and like I've betrayed my husband. I kissed another man. Not just any man - his brother.

I slide off the dresser and grab my nightie off the floor, clutching it against my body as I search around the room for my dressing gown.

What am I going to do?

How am I going to explain this to my husband?

Just then - Masaccio walks into the room.

"Mas - I'm so sorry. I didn't know - I thought it was you - I kissed your brother - I'm so sorry - please."

I know I'm rambling, and I can't seem to control the words streaming out of my mouth, but absolute panic has consumed me. I'm terrified he will leave me. What if he asks for a divorce?

Mas is staring at me with a cold look in his eyes. His eyes are trailing up and down my naked body in disgust as I try to hide behind the tiny scrap of fabric I am holding.

"How did you know it was my brother?"

"Because I know you. Will you ever forgive me? I promise you I stopped as soon as I realized."

"But what was it that gave it away?"

I swallow hard. He must be furious.

"I - I don't know. I could just tell it wasn't you. The way he moved. The way he kissed. His laugh—" I don't know how to explain this.

Mas tilts his head as though he is curious.

My eyes narrow towards him. This is not the reaction I was expecting. He doesn't *seem* angry.

"Wait - did you - did you *know*?" the words spill from my mouth in disbelief.

He doesn't reply.

"Masaccio, did you *know* your brother was in here with me?" I ask again, more anger than fear now.

He shrugs.

He fucking *shrugs*. And suddenly I am so angry that I want to tear his skin off.

"You sent your brother in here? You planned this? What the fuck is wrong with you?"

Tears are streaming down my cheeks. "Were you testing me? What kind of sick and fucked up game is this?" I can't stop shouting.

"Stop shouting. Calm the fuck down." He snaps.

"I won't calm down. How dare you tell me to calm down after sending your brother into my room—" I don't even know what to say. I don't understand what is going on.

Why the hell is he looking at me like that?

Mas steps closer to me and reaches out to grab my nightie.

He yanks it out of my hands and tosses it to the floor.

"So, you know me so well that you could tell the difference between me and my identical brother? My father took years to tell us apart, but you can tell the difference?"

I step away from him, covering my body with my hands self-consciously.

"I —I know you, Mas. Because you are the one I'm —" I swallow hard. He's the one I fell in love with. Of course, I know him.

"I'm the one you want." He takes another step towards me and his body presses against mine.

I can feel his cock. Rigid. Bulging against his pants.

"I'm the one you want." He repeats, deeper, a growl that rumbles from his chest and vibrate against me.

"Y—yes." I stammer.

He lifts me off the floor, onto the dresser, pressing his hips between my legs and forcing them open.

He grabs my neck and pulls my mouth against his, kissing me hard.

Instantly my body lights with electricity.

This is how I knew.

This feeling.

This intensity.

This is what was missing.

My breath catches in my throat as Mas pulls his shirt off and yanks his pants open while he continues to kiss me.

Then, standing naked in front of me, he leans back to let his eyes roam my body.

"You are beautiful, Leora."

The way he says my name sends butterflies racing through me.

He lifts me in his arms and carries me to the bed. I can feel his cock pressed against my pussy. I am nervous, excited - flooded with emotions as he lies down over me.

"I hope you can handle this." He whispers against my ear.

I'm unable to speak as I feel him pressing his cock harder against me.

He slides inside me. I feel my pussy stretching open around his cock.

"Oh." I gasp, trying to adjust to the sheer size of him.

He doesn't wait or say anything. Instead, he pushes deeper into me.

I gasp and arch my back. I can't tell the difference between pain and pleasure at this point.

He slides deeper into me, and I cry out, loudly, not even bothering to hold it back.

He wraps his hand around my jaw, tilting my head back as he moves back and forth over me.

The pain intensifies for a few seconds, but then the pleasure takes over.

I spread my legs wider, wanting to feel everything as he moves faster.

My entire body relaxes when the pleasure becomes the only thing I can feel, and I dig my finger nails into his back.

He fucks me even harder. His hand moves from my jaw to my throat as his fingers press against my skin.

I can barely breathe.

My legs are shaking, I can't control it. I can't control anything that is happening in my body because he has complete control over me.

I hear him grunt and growl as he slams into me - his cock buried so far inside me it feels as though I might tear in two.

But despite that intensity - I still want more. I want more of him, everything.

I arch my back and press my pussy up towards him as pleasure shoots up my spine.

My body shudders beneath him.

And then it slams into me, wave after wave of the most intense orgasm I have ever felt in my life.

He thrusts forward one last time and I feel him explode inside me.

He sighs, lifting himself off the bed, grabbing his clothes, and leaving the room.

I stare after him, not sure what just happened.

He didn't say a word to me. He just left.

I grab my duvet and pull it up over my body.

Is that normal? Is that what all guys do?

My heart pulls tight in my chest. I thought - maybe - I thought he would sleep in my bed. But I know he prefers to sleep alone.

That's all it is. He just wants to sleep alone.

Everything has changed now - he's made love to me. Tomorrow is going to be a new day, a new relationship.

I grin as I flop down onto my bed, snuggling against my pillow. This is the first step for us to become closer.

My heart flip flops.

I am so in love with him. I can't wait for him to show me how he feels about me too.

CHAPTER ELEVEN
Masaccio

I push myself off the bed almost as soon as it's over.

I don't know what's wrong with me - I feel - overwhelmed. I feel weird.

Glancing down at her, for a moment, I can't help but think how beautiful she is.

But then I shake my head, forcing the thought away. I turn to grab my things and leave the room. I just need to get out of here. That's all.

I got caught up in the moment. The idea of someone wanting me so intensely that they could tell the difference between my identical twin brother and myself - someone I don't even know very well -

She didn't just want to experience losing her virginity - she wanted *me*.

No one else.

I sigh heavily. Forcing the air out of my lungs as though I am trying to throw these ridiculous thoughts out with it.

That felt too good.

That's the problem.

It felt fucking incredible and almost as soon as I walk away from her - I want more.

I storm into my room and close the door.

Dammit.

I should never have done that.

I've made a massive mistake giving in to that urge.

But fuck. She was standing there, angry - angry because it wasn't me kissing her. She made me feel - something.

And her body. That shred of fabric she was holding up against herself hid nothing.

It was just impulse.

I acted on impulse and did not think that through.

But it's fine.

I'll get some sleep and tomorrow things should be more settled.

She got what she wanted - and now she can step back and leave me the hell alone.

Besides, she'll probably still be mad as hell about Tuomo going into her room first. She might just be over me which would be a relief.

All night I toss and turn in my bed.

I have these stupid images in my head of being in her bed. I can't stop thinking about it.

When I fall asleep, I dream about her, sitting on top of me, rocking her hips over me as she throws her hair back.

"Mas?" Her voice drags me from my dream into the real world. I blink, my face pressed against my pillow.

"What?" I groan, without turning towards her. I'm so tired. I hardly slept at all. Why is she in my room?

"I made you breakfast in bed." She says, sweet as ever.

"I'm not hungry." I mumble. Even though I'm starving.

"Ok, I'll just leave it here for you."

I hear her putting the tray down on my bedside table.

Then her footsteps fade out of the room, down the passage.

I sit up, looking over at the food.

Coffee. Creamy and dark.

I reach for it right away.

She made toast with bacon, egg and fried tomato.

It looks so damn good.

I tilt my head, listening for her, but she's gone.

So, I pick up the tray and eat the breakfast.

I carry it down to the kitchen when I'm done and put the plate in the washer so she can't see it. For some reason I don't want her to know that I enjoyed it.

She comes into the kitchen while I'm making my second cup of coffee.

I feel her hands, tracing over my sides from behind. She presses her body against my back, hugging me. "I can make that for you?" Heat spreads through my body at her touch. My cock stirs, eager for a repeat of last night.

I step away from her, getting the milk out of the fridge even though I don't need it yet.

"No, I can make my coffee. You don't need to make me breakfast in the morning either. Thank you. But I can sort myself out."

She giggles and then replies.

"I enjoyed making breakfast for you. Don't be silly. What did you want to do today?" She slips her arms back around me now that I'm standing back at the coffee machine with the milk on the counter next to me, I have nowhere to run now. No reason to turn away. I clench my jaw, holding back an annoyed snarl. My body wants her so badly. My mind wishes she would leave me the hell alone.

"I don't know what *I'm* doing today. You can do whatever you want."

"I thought maybe we could go for a walk or go out somewhere?"

"No." I say.

She shrugs. "That's ok. I know it was last minute. We can make plans for another time. What are you doing for dinner tonight?"

Is she really so blind to my more than obvious body language? I am not interested. Do I need to spell it out for her? I turn to stare down at her, my eyes narrowed, nothing comforting or soft about my glare.

"I don't know what *I'm* doing for dinner tonight, Leora. You must do whatever you want. Don't worry about what I have planned."

"Ok." She smiles. But still seems un-phased when she leans her head against my shoulder.

Oh, my fuck. I need to get away from her.

"I forgot. I have a meeting. I'll get coffee on the way." I say, pushing away from the kitchen counter and walking out because I can't handle how clingy she's being *and how it's making my body heat with anticipation*.

She clearly assumes that because of last night we are somehow super close now.

She is the most naïve and clueless person I've ever met.

I don't actually know how to handle it. So, I think the best thing is if I just get out of here for the day. She can simmer down. Maybe get the message while I'm gone.

Dammit.

It really doesn't help that I am so fucking attracted to her.

I get dressed in a hurry, then rush downstairs to grab my car keys. She isn't here, thank goodness, she must be in her room.

I pull the door closed behind myself and even though I do not know where I'm going, I'm happy to be out of the house where I can breathe a little.

It's late when I get back home, almost nine o'clock. I made a point of staying out until after dinner time, sitting at the bar alone having a beer and wondering what the hell is going on in my life.

I push the front door open and the rich aroma of roast lamb rushes over me.

It smells incredible.

I peak my head into the kitchen, relieved that she isn't there. She must have eaten and gone up to her room already.

I scratch around in the kitchen, not finding the food, wondering where she would have stored the leftovers.

"Odd." I mumble. Maybe she left it on the dining room table for the housekeeper to sort out in the morning.

I make my way through the living room and into the dining room.

She's sitting at the table, smiling, wearing the most gorgeous tight red dress I have ever seen.

Her hair is falling loose over her shoulders and the entire room is lit with candles, flickering and casting moving shadows around the room.

On the table she has set up two placemats. The roast lamb is on a board in the center, and surrounding it are potatoes roasted to crisped perfection, green beans tossed with garlic mushrooms and butternut squares.

My mouth is watering - for the food and for her in that incredible dress.

"Mas - um - surprise." She says with a shy giggle.

My lips curl in a snarl as I bite back my annoyance.

"I thought I told you not to worry about me for dinner?"

"You did, but I really wanted to just - do something nice - to surprise you." She stands up and walks around the table towards me. Her hips swaying and the candlelight making her skin glow.

She slips her hands around my waist and lifts her head as though she wants to kiss me.

I turn my head away.

"I'm going to bed." I mutter, dark and moody.

"Oh, but—"

"Night, Leora." I step away from her and hurry out of the dining room.

My stomach churns in anger as I walk away from the incredible dinner she prepared. But how can I sit there in romantic candlelight and eat with her? What kind of message would that give her?

CHAPTER TWELVE
Leora

The sun is backing down on my skin as I lie on the sun lounger by the pool. Alone at home as usual, wondering where my husband is. He spends a lot of time out of the house. Especially after the night we made love. And of course, that hasn't happened again.

At least the sun is out in full force today and I can relax and soak up the warmth on my skin. I stretch my legs out and wiggle my toes.

I'm feeling really defeated. Like I should just give up.

I've been trying so hard to spend time with him, to have conversations, to sit and have a coffee even - just that - in the mornings. But he makes it so difficult. He's always rushing off somewhere or pushing me away - and it's starting to really hurt. I still don't understand why he's being this way. And of course, I can't ask him because he never has time to talk about anything - never mind serious issues.

Every single time he turns his face away from me when I try to kiss him it breaks a piece of my heart away. Cracks form and spread like an ache that I can't ignore.

I sigh and pull my sunglasses up over the top of my head, blinking into the bright afternoon light.

I can't keep this up for much longer.

At some point I am going to have to be honest with myself and accept that he just doesn't like me. What would that mean though? What would it mean for me - and my life - to live with a man who doesn't even like the sight of me?

No. Something is going on and all I have to do is try to understand it. If I can understand it, I can work out how to communicate with him.

I bite my lower lip. Dammit. My heart won't let me just give up like that - so I won't.

I really love him.

I was so excited when I found out that I was going to marry him - I thought the universe was giving me a gift - but now - now what am I supposed to do.

At the back of my eyes, I feel tears stinging and threatening to spill.

No. I won't give up just yet. There must be something I can do to bring him closer to me.

"Hello." The sing song voice drifts through the house towards me. I roll onto my side to peak around the back of the sun lounger.

"Dalila - hello." I call out from the pool side.

"Oh, there you are." She walks out of the house towards me. "I brought us summer treats. It's so hot today I wanted to come over and swim, but I see you already had that idea." She laughs, setting her things down next to the other lounger she pulls her sundress over her head, revealing her pretty pink bikini. "Nevio is swamped at work and I've been getting bored at home alone." She hands me a vodka cocktail in a soda can.

"What's this?" I ask, sitting up a little.

"Pre-made strawberry something or other. They taste amazing." She cracks a can open for herself and sips on it.

"How have you been?" She asks as I sip mine.

"Mm. This is amazing. Thanks. I guess I've been ok."

"You guess?" she eyes me over the top of her sunglasses.

"Yes, you know, it's the whole getting bored home alone thing - and just - Masaccio in general—"

"What do you mean? Is he working too much? Do you guys not get to spend time together?"

"I don't even think he's working that much to be honest. I think - I think he's just trying to get away from me."

"Nonsense. Don't say that." She pouts her lower lip out a little.

"I'm not trying to be weird - I mean it. I don't think he likes me too much."

She sits up and turns her body towards me. "Well, why - like what is he doing or not doing to make you feel that way?"

"You know - I've been trying everything to connect with him. I want to spend time with him so that we can get to know each other. The other night I made us a candle lit dinner - he refused to eat it. He even looked angry about it."

"Why wouldn't he eat it?"

"I do not know. And every time I put my arm around him, he finds a reason to move away from me. And he won't kiss me. I mean never mind anything else a husband and wife *could* do - he won't even *kiss* me."

This time I can't hold the tears back. Saying it all out loud make it so much more real and hearing my own words make me realize just how much it has been hurting me to feel this constant push from him.

"He just - he just constantly rejects me. It's really hurting me." I admit.

I can't believe I just told his sister all of that. But I don't have anyone else to talk to. I can't talk to Mas about it, and I guess I just really needed to talk.

"Oh no, sweetie. I'm so sorry to hear that. You know - Mas has always been the hardest one to get through to. He has a massive heart. But he can seem so cold. It's because of the way we were raised." She says, leaning back in the sun lounger.

"What do you mean? How was he raised?"

"My dad is not the most affectionate guy on the planet. In fact - he showed no emotions at all. You know Mas is the oldest, so my dad has been sort of training him ever since he was a kid - his entire purpose has always been to take over from my dad in the family business. I don't think Mas has ever felt or experienced love. I don't think he knows what it is."

"Really? He's never felt love?"

She smiles a tight smile and shrugs. "He had it the hardest, I think. Dealing with my dad."

"What do you think I should do?" I ask, rolling my entire body towards her because I desperately need advice from someone who knows Mas as well as she does.

"I think - you should give him a chance. Maybe he's scared. He really is a good guy. He's a great brother. He's stubborn and annoying—" she laughs, "but I love him to bits. If you just give him a chance to open up to you - I'm sure he will."

She sounds so sincere and sure of her own advice. Maybe I was giving up too soon.

Maybe I just need to keep trying for a little longer.

My heart feels so much lighter sitting out at the pool with Dalila on this beautiful sunny day.

She hands me another strawberry cocktail and then tips her own towards me. "Cheers." She says.

"Cheers." I reply, smiling for the first time in a few days.

I think everything is going to be ok.

I will show him what love really is. I can teach him how to love.

He deserves that. Everyone does.

And I want to do that for him.

Dalila and I lay by the pool all afternoon. When Mas gets home, we are both a little tipsy and our skin is rosy and pink.

She hears him coming through and turns to wave at him.

"Hey brother." She says giggling.

"What are you two doing?" He asks, looking down on both of us.

It doesn't go unnoticed how his eyes take in my body, wearing nothing but my blue bikini. I can see he likes it.

I really do just need to give him a little more time. That's all.

"I was just leaving." Dalila stands up, stretching, then pulls her summer dress over her head. She leans over the sun lounger and hugs me. "Thanks so much for a fun afternoon sweetie. I'll see you soon."

"Bye babe. Thanks - for everything." I grin.

Mas turn to walk her out. I hear them chatting away.

A little fire of hope has been sparked inside me all over again and I feel excited about the possibilities of everything.

I smile as I watch the sun beginning to set.

Soon the air will get a little cooler and I'll go inside. But right now, I'm so relaxed, and feeling happier than I have all week, so I'm just going to enjoy this moment.

CHAPTER THIRTEEN
Masaccio

"Alright - tell me what your problem is?" Dalila insists as soon as we are out of earshot from Leora.

"Huh? What are you talking about? I don't have a problem." I shrug, feeling defensive.

"Well, then what's going on with you? Why are you being such an asshole to Leora? She's your wife but you don't even want to hug her—" He says.

I sigh and roll my eyes.

"Dalila, firstly, it's none of your business - secondly she isn't a real wife."

"What the hell. How can you say that?"

Dalila looks upset. She glares at me with her hand on her hip.

"You know what I mean. This whole thing - it's fake. It's just for show. The sooner Leora realizes that the better it will be for both of us."

"Mas - it doesn't have to be fake. Just because it wasn't what you wanted, not something you chose, doesn't mean it has to suck. If you just got to know her - maybe spend a little time with her. She's a really sweet — "

"No."

I want her to leave now. I don't want to discuss this.

I turn to walk towards the front door, but Dalila grabs my arm, pulling me back to face her.

"No. You can't just walk away like that. Talk to me. What is it you don't like about her?"

Her question is really straight forward - to the point - and it catches me completely off guard.

What is it I don't like about Leora?

My mind is racing to find an answer to give to my sister. One that makes sense. Anything. I can't come up with anything at all.

"Well? What's wrong with her, Mas? Why don't you want to spend time with her?" Dalila can tell she's put me in an awkward position. She can tell I have no real reason to dislike her.

"It's not that simple." I say after an awkward silence.

She punches my shoulder, scrunching her nose. "It *is that simple dumbass.*" She huffs. "It's as simple as at least giving her a chance. You can't just ignore your wife for the rest of your life you know." She rolls her eyes.

"Ok. Ok, you've had your say - you can go now."

She reaches out and touches my arm. Her eyes are softer now. Caring. "Please Mas, promise me you'll at least give this a proper chance?"

"Fine. I promise."

Dalila wraps her arms around my waist and hugs me tight. I can smell sunscreen and strawberries on her. She smells like summer.

Guilt washes through me because in so many ways I know my sister is right.

I haven't even stopped to ask myself that question - to ask myself what I don't like about Leora.

I sigh, giving Dalila a one-armed hug, then pushing her towards the front door.

"Go home already." I say in a teasing voice.

She skips ahead and pushes the door open, then turns to look back at me. She narrows her eyes and tilts her head, throwing me a look that says *you promised*.

I wave and roll my eyes. "Yeah, yeah." I say before she disappears out to her car.

Maybe I really do need to give Leora a chance.

It's so difficult though.

I never wanted this.

I walk through the living room, standing at the patio doors I look out towards the pool - to where Leora is lying in that bikini, her long shapely legs stretched out in front of her - I turn away from the incredible view, not liking the way my body is never in my control around her.

I like to be in control, but she turns me on in an instant and I'm worried -

I'm worried that I'll sleep with her again and it will just get more intense and awkward.

I head upstairs to my bedroom.

I'll have to give it some time, think it through and decide the best way to handle this situation.

The next morning, I leave the house before Leora is awake.

I do actually have work to do. But I've decided that I will at least have a short conversation with her tonight.

Perhaps ask how her day was. Something normal. Easy going.

I don't want to over think it.

I'll just keep it as simple as possible and give myself a chance to get to know her before I decide anything.

We might at least be friends.

That evening when I get back Leora has made another candle lit dinner.

Walk into the house and smell the Bolognese straight away.

One thing I can vouch for is that her cooking is incredible.

"Mas." She sounds excited as she rushes over to greet me. "How was your day? Did you get everything done that you needed to do?" She wraps her arms around my waist, and I force myself to hug her back even though it feels stiff and formal.

"I had a good day, thanks. How was yours?" I sound a bit robotic. Why am I so terrible at this?

"It was super. Come on. I've just finished setting the table and the foods about to come out the oven. You have perfect timing."

"Can I help with anything?" I ask, following her to the kitchen. She turns around and chases me away. "No, I'm making dinner for you - you've been at work all day. Go sit down. Relax."

I nod. Feeling awkward. Getting chased out of my kitchen is not something I appreciate.

I suppose she is trying to make a nice gesture. That's all.

I head through to the dining room, grabbing a drink on the way.

The room is set up with those same candles flickering like a festive little party.

I sit down, not relaxed at all, taking big sips of my drinking hoping the alcohol will help me through this dinner.

Leora comes through carrying a dish of bolognas with crunch cheese grilled on top. Damn it smells so good.

She sets it down on the table.

I don't wait to let her dish up for me because I don't want her to do me anymore favors than she already has. Just now she will be expecting things in return.

Standing up I take the spoon and dish up for her, then myself.

"Thanks." She grins, taking a seat.

We eat in silence for a while - me trying to figure out how to start a conversation with someone I don't know at all - who is living in my house - her with a watchful eye on me.

"Do you like it?" She asks.

"It's incredible."

I eat faster than I should because while I am enjoying the food I am not enjoying this shared moment. It's too much.

I asked her how her day was and that was pretty much all the conversation I can handle with her.

She is now chatting away about the recipe and how her grandmother handed it down to her father and he taught her when she was young and how much she loves cooking like it's an act of love - and on and on and on.

Watching her while she twirls spaghetti onto her fork, looking down at her plate, I notice again how beautiful she is. Her face is lit up with enthusiasm as she shares this story with me, even though I am not really listening.

She's animated and cheerful.

She makes it look easy - to make conversation - to be relaxed.

I sigh and lean back in my chair.

"Thank you, Leora, that was good. I am going to head up and shower and then call it a night."

"Oh, wait, um - before you go—"

She reaches under the table, to the empty chair next to her, and pulls up a box.

It's wrapped in black satin paper with a black ribbon around it.

It's not big. But it makes me incredibly uncomfortable.

"I bought you a present." She smiles, handing it over the table to me.

I stand up and take it from her, letting my arm hang at my side, gripping the gift in my hand.

I never know how to react when someone gives me a gift.

"Thank you - good night." I turn away from the table and hurry from the room.

CHAPTER FOURTEEN
Leora

I giggle as he hurries out of the living room. He is one of those people who gets super awkward when they receive gifts. I think I almost saw him blushing now. He looked nervous. He couldn't get out of here fast enough.

I think he'll take it up to his bedroom and open it in private.

But I am one of those people who loves to watch people's expressions when they open gifts. I love to see their faces and if I made the right choice.

I thought long and hard about what to get him and after a little bit of snooping in his room this morning, I found his watch collection. A very impressive selection of rare watches - and so I hunted down a very rare, limited-edition watch - from his favorite brand. I know it's his favorite brand because more than half of the watches in his collection are that brand.

I can't help myself.

I have to see his face when he opens it.

I hurry up the stairs, running. I press my body against the wall and peak around the doorframe.

He is sitting on his bed, taking off his shoes. The gift box is next to him on the bed.

I grin.

He'll definitely open it now.

He slides his shoes under his bed and sits staring at the box for a moment. Then he picks it up. Standing.

"What the fuck did she do this for?" he mutters angrily. My heart sinks. Does he not like the fact that I got him a gift? Why would it upset him?

"She really doesn't get it." He murmurs, then walks over to his dresser and pulls the bottom drawer open, tossing the black box into the drawer - unopened. He stands up and kicks the drawer closed.

My heart is in my throat and tears and stabbing the back of my eyes. He turns around and I duck out of the doorway, out of sight.

I hear him carry on getting undressed.

Then I bolt downstairs, needing to get away because I can't hold back the tears anymore and I don't need him to hear me crying.

Sitting in the living room with all the lights off - the dark is bringing me a quiet, lonely comfort.

I'm thinking about everything. Everything that happened since I first kissed Mas.

Everything that I misread - misunderstood or made assumptions about.

And basically, I realize, I have made the wrong assumptions about every little moment between us.

He could not have been clearer.

He is one hundred percent not interested in me.

This marriage is for show. Nothing more. And he has zero intention of even trying to let it mean more.

We are not real husband and wife.

I fold my knees against my chest and rest my face against my knees as I cry.

I'm so naïve. I'm so immature. I know nothing about love - and now - I'll never ever learn about it because I am married to a man who will never love me.

I cry for over an hour. I guess I knew all along. You can be as delusional as you like, but somewhere in the back of your mind, in the bottom of your heart - you know the truth.

I could feel he wasn't really into me.

I was just wishful.

When I can feel my eyes are too dry to cry anymore and I am too tired to keep them open, I drag myself upstairs to my bedroom.

From now on - I will stop being that annoying, pestering, delusional girl.

I will accept things for what they really are.

The sooner I embrace this the better it will be for both of us.

I lie in bed with a broken heart.

I can't sleep.

My mind is fighting with itself. My heart is begging me not to give up.

But all that is happening is that I am getting more and more hurt over a man who doesn't want me. I don't deserve to feel this broken, this worthless, this rejected.

By my husband.

Just before I fall asleep, I promise myself to close my heart and rather be numb towards him that risk any more pain.

It's for the best.

Life isn't a fairytale. And I am not a princess.

Over the next week I do my absolute best to stay out of his way.

I spend a lot of time out of the house too. Shopping. Walking around the city garden. Visiting friends. Browsing bookshops. It doesn't really matter. I just need to distract myself and create distance between Mas and me.

When I am home and he's around, I try not to be in the same room as him.

Sometimes, in the morning it's awkward as we are making coffee at the same time and it's impossible not to exchange a few words.

But I keep my answers short and get out of his way as quickly as I can.

I don't even think he has noticed. If he has, it's a relief for him to not have to fake being nice. Not that he was very good at being nice. Even in a fake way. If I am brutally honest with myself, he hasn't been nice to me once. And I was blindly going about thinking I was in love with him.

I sigh as I carry my coffee cup up to my bedroom.

I was in love with him.

But I had to turn it off. I had to block my heart and stop my feelings.

It still hurts. I can still feel it there - the hope - but I have to drown it.

Nothing good can come of being in love with Masaccio Vece.

I drink my coffee and get ready for another day where I will leave the house to get out of his way. "Is this my life now?" I say, talking to no one at all. "Is this what the rest of my life is going to be like? Married to a man who doesn't even want to speak to me - not even comfortable in my home—lonely—" I stop talking because if I carry on, I will cry again.

This sucks.

This is the worst possible outcome I could ever have imagined when I was told I would marry Masaccio Vece.

My *dream* man.

I pick up my handbag, sip the last of my coffee, and head downstairs to my car.

"Where are you off to?" Masaccio's voice comes from behind me as I reach the bottom of the staircase.

"Just out for a bit." I say coolly.

"You're hardly around anymore." He walks down the stairs and stands close to me. Too close. I can smell his cologne. I can feel the heat from his skin.

It annoys me.

I want to roll my eyes. *'Oh, you noticed I've been going out a lot lately did you.' I'm surprised.*

But instead, I just nod. The less I engage with him the better. I take a small step away from him, trying not to be enticed by his scent. Or his body.

It even hurts to look at him because I still think he is the most gorgeous man alive.

No point though. There is *no point* to any of this.

"Will you be home for dinner?" he asks, and I can't figure out why he's still talking to me.

"I'm not sure." I say, shrugging. Then before he can stretch this awkward moment out any further, I turn towards the front door again and wave my hand over my shoulder. "Bye." I say, walking away. Now he doesn't have to pretend to be polite and I don't have to suffer through another moment with the man I wish I was allowed to be in love with.

"Oh - bye." He says.

I hurry out of the front door. Biting my lower lip as I rush towards my car. He is standing at the front door watching me - why? Why is he even interested in what I'm doing?

As I pull out of the driveway, I make a point of not looking back towards him. I don't want to know if he's still there watching or not. Either way it will just hurt me.

CHAPTER FIFTEEN
Masaccio

Leora rushes past my bedroom door, towards the stairs, carrying her handbag. She is leaving again. She's hardly ever home lately.

I stand up and rush to follow her.

Standing at the top of the stairs I talk because I need to grab her attention before she's out the door and gone for the entire day again.

"Where are you off to?" I call out as she steps off the stairway.

She doesn't turn to face me.

"Just out for a bit." Her voice is bland and void of emotion.

"You're hardly around anymore."

I walk down the stairs towards her, and she is forced to turn and face me.

I stand close, almost pushing her up against curved railing of the staircase.

She looks annoyed by my comment as I stare down at her. She won't make eye contact.

This is not like the Leora I was getting used to.

That Leora was talkative and playful. She used to try to reach out towards me sometimes or steal a hug in the kitchen while I was making coffee.

For the past week Leora has been leaving without saying goodbye and staying out for the entire day - I don't even know what she's been up to because she doesn't even speak to me when she is home.

I've been eating dinner alone because she eats in her room and the only evidence, I have of how she's staying busy is an empty bookshop packet or a take-away coffee mug - it's kind of ridiculous that I live with her but - it doesn't seem like I live with anyone.

She takes a step away from me and I feel I need to make more conversation otherwise she will just leave. "Will you be home for dinner?"

"I'm not sure." She shrugs, nonchalant, disinterested. Then she turns away from me, waves her hand in the air and shouts. "Bye."

"Oh - bye." I stammer, following her to the door.

I don't even know where she's going or when she will be back.

Shouldn't I know where my wife is going?

I watch her as she climbs into her car, not turning to look at me again, not even when she pulls out of the long driveway and turn out onto the street.

I sigh.

I don't know why I've been feeling so bland these last few days.

The house has been so quiet - it feels empty.

Leora has created quite a distance between us. I've noticed. Of course, I've noticed. It's impossible not to notice.

The first day it was pleasant. Peaceful. I thought she was just having a quiet day. But then it happened again the next day, and I was confused. I tried to talk to her while we were both making coffee that morning - but she was off.

I tried to talk to her one evening after she was out all day, and she gave me one worded answers before carrying her dinner up to her room and eating behind a closed door.

Her bedroom door is always closed now.

I eat alone.

I have coffee alone.

It feels like I live alone.

And - I don't like it.

So, now it's been a week. And I hate to admit it - but I miss how annoying she was.

I miss the sound of her laughter. I feel like I should have paid more attention to what she was saying when she was telling me stories.

I miss her. It's so weird to admit that.

And it's annoying me.

I think I know what to do though.

Just to get her to stop avoiding me so much and spend a tiny bit of time with me. I'll pull her own trick on her. A candlelight dinner.

She's made it twice for me so it's obviously something she enjoys.

I'll do the same for her.

Picking up the phone I message the chef who should arrive later today.

> Me: Dimitri, I need you to make something special for tonight. Three courses. Main dish must be lobster. I want the dining room to look like a five-star restaurant.

> Dimitri: yes, sir. I'll stop at the market on my way to you and pick up fresh ingredients. You will be very impressed with your dinner. I assure you. How many guests?

> Me: It is a dinner for my wife and me. Dinner at eight.

I might not be as good at cooking as she is - but I can still make this great.

Leora arrives home just before eight and I make sure I am waiting at the door to open it for her.

"What?" she jumps as I pull it open as she reaches for the handle on the other side.

"What are you doing here?" She asks, a little out of breath from her fright.

"Welcome home. I've had a special dinner prepared for us. I hope you haven't eaten yet."

She bites her lower lip. I love it when she does that.

"Um - I haven't. But I'm tired."

"Don't worry. I won't keep you up late. You have to eat something."

I take her shopping bags from her and set them aside, hang her coat on the hook near the door and lead her through to the dining room with my hand resting on her lower back. Sparks flying from my fingertips against her skin.

A soft gasp escapes her lips when she sees the candles and the setting. Leora hesitates in the doorway of the dining room. "What is this, Mas?" She asks.

"It's dinner. A small thank you for the dinners you made me." I gently push her into the room and pull out a chair for her. She sits down and I take a seat next to her.

Our legs are touching beneath the table and it's reminding my body what it was like to be with her. How she felt wrapped in my arms.

"It's just that…" Her words trail off as the chef carries the starter in and plates it for us.

Muscles in white wine and garlic sauce and oysters in vodka and chili.

It looks incredible.

"Thank you." Leora smiles at Dimitri.

The starter is amazing, but Leora is hardly talking at all.

I can see I am going to have to encourage her to open up and chat. Strange, as every other dinner we've had she has talked easily and freely.

"Have you been enjoying your days wherever you end up going?"

She looks up from her plate, eyeing me.

"I'm not up to anything. If that's what you are asking. I just go walk around the garden, or the book shop. Sometimes the mall."

"Oh - no - that's not what I meant." I clear my throat. I had not intended for it to come across as an interrogation. "No, I just wanted to know if you have been enjoying your time? Um—you haven't been home much—"

"I know." She says rather coldly.

Dimitri arrives with our main course. The lobster - done in garlic butter with lemon slices.

She smiles at Dimitri again. She hasn't smiled at me since the last dinner she made me. It was over a week ago.

She looks down at her plate. Not saying a word, she enjoys her lobster. But she doesn't look happy at all. My heart pulls tight in my chest. I don't like this version of her. I want the real Leora back. I don't understand what made her so cold and distant.

"Leora?"

She looks up at me, waiting without saying a word. Her bright eyes look sharp and intense, but not welcoming. They look hostile. I wish I could read her mind. It would make life so much easier for me. I take a deep breath.

"Leora - what's wrong?" I ask.

She tilts her head to the side. Her brows knotted. "Nothing is wrong." Her answer is too clipped. To short.

Her eyes look empty. The usual sparkle is no longer there. She almost looks like a hollow version of herself.

"Something is wrong." I say more forcefully. She can't just deny it like that. "You don't speak to me. You are never home. You don't eat with me—"

She drops her fork and glares at me.

CHAPTER SIXTEEN
Leora

I drop my fork and glare at him. I can feel the anger flooding from my eyes towards him.

What game is he playing by asking me this?

Why the hell does he care? Why is he questioning me about these things?

"Why does it matter if I speak to you or not? Why do you care if I am home or not?" I snap, annoyed that I even had to sit at this table and eat dinner with him because being around him is still too difficult for me.

His eyes darken and his jaw muscles feather.

"What the hell do you mean by that?" He asks.

"I mean - with all due respect - why does it *matter* if I am home or out? What difference does it make to you? It's not like you enjoy my company. It's not like you enjoy the dinners I make for you and it's certainly not like you enjoyed it when I made a fool of myself trying to hug you on those random occasions." I fold my arms across my chest, repeating over and over in my mind that I will not cry. I will *not* cry.

"Leora—" he stammers, but he does not know how to handle my outburst of truth. He's only met the happy version of me - and the quiet version. He's never had to deal with my anger.

I never even wanted to talk about this. I'm angry he put me in this position because even if I pretend, I'm ok with this - I'm not. I'm still hurting. I've gone quiet to deal with the pain - and now he's forcing it out of me. It's unfair. Why can't he see that?

My fists are clenching and unclenching where they are lying on top of the table. My eyes feel like they are shooting spears out of them as I glare at him.

I can't do this now. I'm too emotional. It will not end well.

I stand up to leave. Wanting to get away before he sees me crying. And not wanting to embarrass myself more than I already have around him.

But he stands up as well and glares at me with intensity. "Sit down. We are not finished eating yet."

The way he speaks to me is like a slap in the face. What is *he* so angry about? What right does he have to be upset just because I am doing what he wanted all along?

But I don't argue. The chef has put so much effort into the meal and on his behalf, I sit back down. Besides, I'm not keen to start an actual fight - and it feels as though we are about to.

I take a deep breath, trying to calm myself.

Masaccio sits down too, with a heavy sigh. He doesn't seem to understand. Which makes no sense to me. How can someone put effort into achieving something - then be upset when they get it?

When he speaks again, I can see he has attempted to soften his expression and calm his voice.

"Leora, I am just trying to find out what is going on with you. You haven't been yourself lately. The past week or so. You look - unhappy. You can talk to me you know. You can tell me what's on your mind. I mean - the first few weeks you were here I couldn't get you to stop talking—and now—" he grins and shakes his head. "Now, where are those long stories?"

I take a deep breath, trying to figure out how the hell to answer him.

He never even listened to my long stories. I bet you if I asked him a simple question about anything I've told him about myself or my life - he wouldn't be able to answer. So why does he want more stories now?

"Look, Mas, I *know* I've been different this past week. I'm doing it as a choice. Not by accident. It isn't something that is easy for me - but I had to accept the reality of this situation and behave according to truth instead of some stupid delusional idea I had in my head."

I guess that's as blunt and honest as I can be.

"What?" He blurts out. He has no idea what I mean.

Fuck sakes. I bite my lip, hard, to stop myself from yelling at him.

I just want to go to my room and be alone.

I sigh and try to explain a different way.

"I came into this marriage feeling *excited*. Hopeful. Like a naïve little girl thinking I'd have this 'happy ever after' moment. But in the past week I have fully accepted and processed and come to understand - that is not the case. You've made it more than clear that this marriage is *nothing but a show*. A business deal or whatever you want to call it. So, I stopped being pathetic and grasping for your attention when you clearly didn't want to give it to me. I stopped asking for something that was never going to happen. Because lets be honest - all I was doing was embarrassing myself."

I feel the tears stinging my eyes and reach for my wine glass just so that I have something to do. Something to distract me from the ache that is growing in my heart because he is forcing me to talk about this.

I can't even look at him.

"Leora, why would you say that—I—I—" he is acting so surprised. It doesn't make sense. How the fuck can he be surprised.

"You what?" I spit my words out at him because I'm becoming too emotional.

I was doing so well turning myself numb this past week and I was not prepared to open up like this tonight.

And how the hell can he sit there and pretend he didn't know?

"Mas, are you trying to tell me you didn't treat me like I was just pestering you? Do you want to lie to my face and try to tell me you made me feel welcome here? That you treated me like you wanted me around? Like you *enjoyed my company?*" my voice is straining as I try to hold back my tears again. Angry tears. Angry, hurt, frustrated tears because he can't be that cold.

"Leora - just take a deep breath, calm down—"

"Calm down?" I stand up again, knocking my wine glass over. "I will not calm down. You need to get your facts straight. You need to stop blowing hot and cold and just stick to the cold because you are so good at it. I don't have to sit here listening to you make me sound crazy for how you treated me."

I spin around, marching out of the dining room.

I can't do this. I can't keep my emotions bottled up like this. I thought I was doing fine. I thought I had turned off how I felt about him - but I had just smothered it by staying busy and avoiding him.

I still have feelings for him and just spending this small amount of time with him has reminded me of that.

I need to end this. I need to make my heart go cold and numb once and for all before he destroys me.

I run up the stairs to my bedroom, taking them two at a time.

I rush inside and spin around to slam the door, but to my horror - Mas has followed me.

Dammit. Why?

"Please, just leave me alone." I beg, desperate to just cry in peace.

I try to close the door in his face, but he reaches up and stop it with his one outstretched hand. He's too strong to fight again so I sigh and walk over to my bed to create some distance between us. And he fucking follows me again.

I turn to face him and push him hard in the chest.

"Just leave me alone." I scream, my hurt turning to fire in my body.

He grabs my wrists and yanks me towards him. I gasp when I find myself pressed against his chest. Tears are streaming down my cheeks.

"Mas, please." I beg again.

"I won't leave you alone when you are not ok." He growls, staring down at me.

CHAPTER SEVENTEEN
Masaccio

The tears staining her face are flooding me with guilt.

Her words at the dinner table bit into me like fangs that sank right to my bones. They hurt.

And the reason they hurt so much is that they were all true.

I pushed her away.

I wanted her to leave.

I wanted nothing to do with her when she first arrived here, and I made it clear to her how I felt.

Seeing how badly it affected her though - that is eating away at me. I just didn't think about that part - I didn't think about how she would feel.

She lashes out, trying to free her wrists. I grip tighter.

"I left my *home for you. I came here to live in your house, and I have never once felt welcome.*" She screams. I clench my jaw shut.

"I was happy at home. I was happy with my life. Now its all been taken away from me and I am stuck living with a cold, heartless asshole who doesn't even want me." She's sobbing now and collapsing against me, unable to stand anymore.

I grab her around the waist and pull her against my body.

Anger surges inside me. Anger at myself. Not her.

I grab her jaw and force her face up towards mine.

"Leora." But I don't know what to say. Her eyes are so wide, so innocent, so full of pain. All she wanted was me -

I press my lips against hers, the heat of her skin against mine is all I want to feel right now.

She gasps and tries to pull away, but I grab a handful of her long hair and force her not to move.

I kiss her deeper, more fiercely and feel her give in. Her hands drift up my back and her breathing changes.

My cock is so hard it hurts.

I have never been so turned on in my life.

I step forward, forcing her closer to the bed, then I grab her waist and spin her around, tugging at her jeans and pushing them down her long legs.

She kicks them off.

I grab her top and pull it over her head, leaving her naked. My hands roam around the front of her body, her back pressed against my chest as I cup her ample breasts, playing with her nipples. Pressing my cock against her ass cheeks.

"Wait," she whispers.

I won't wait.

I push her forward, bending her over the bed, kicking my feet against hers to spread her legs wide. Then I pull my own pants open and free my cock.

She tries to turn around to face me and I grab her hair again.

"Don't move." I growl. She arches her back and grips the blankets as she leans forward.

I let her hair go and kneel down behind her, licking my tongue over her tight pink pussy and across her ass.

She shudders with pleasure and deepens the arch of her back - pushing her pussy towards me.

I dip my tongue inside her as I spread her cheeks apart, rocking my face back and forth I fuck her with my tongue, and she moans.

She tastes incredible. I want to lick up every drop of her.

When her legs shake and her moans are getting louder, I stop and stand up, positioning myself behind her.

I rub my cock over her pussy, feeling her warmth - then I thrust into her. So hard she falls forward onto the bed. I move with her, lying on top of her as her face is pressed into the mattress. I keep thrusting hard into her, spreading her legs wide and fucking her from behind. She cries out with each deep thrust of my cock, pushing so hard inside her I can feel her pussy clamping over me.

I wrap my hand around her throat and lift her head up, forcing her to arch her back again because it looks so fucking hot.

Her entire body is shaking as I fuck her faster and faster.

I slip my hand around the front of her body and press my fingers against her clit, rubbing in fast circles as I continue to fuck her with my cock.

She screams, and I feel her pussy suck me deep inside her.

As her orgasm pulses over my cock, I go rigid and explode inside her.

Collapsing on top of her I fight to catch my breath.

Fuck.

She is perfect.

She wiggles a little, letting me know I'm too heavy for her.

I chuckle and roll off, pulling her with me, I wrap my arm around her.

I think I've made it clear that I want her around now.

I think she must have got the message.

But she sighs, sharp and short.

"Please get out." She says, cold and calm.

"What?"

"You can go now - to your own bedroom. I am going to shower and get ready for bed."

"But - don't you want to—"

"No. You can go."

Her coldness is such a shock to me that for a moment I don't respond at all. I feel frozen in place, confused and rejected.

When she pushes away from me and climbs off the bed, walking towards her bathroom, I sit up, shift to the edge of her bed and get off it.

I can't believe she didn't even want to lie there with me for a moment and just cuddle.

I glance towards the bathroom, but the shower is already running.

Walking back to my room I feel so empty. Rejected.

I feel like shit because tonight made me realize something that I have been denying this entire time.

I like my wife.

She's funny, caring, enthusiastic about little things - she brightens up my day - well she used to - until I fucked everything up by being a total fucking asshole.

I flop down onto my bed. I don't even have the energy to shower right now I feel so heavy with regret. I'm not used to all these emotions. I don't understand what they mean.

Lying on my bed staring up at the ceiling I try to think of ways to make it up to her - to make her see I was wrong. That I really want her around.

I've done some serious damage to our relationship. I can't blame her for being upset with me.

The last time I saw smile was the night she gave me that gift - fuck - *that gift*. I didn't even open it.

I stand up and rush to my dresser, pulling open the bottom draw and finding the box upside down near the back. I remember I just tossed it in there as thought it was nothing.

And then I didn't think about it again.

I am filled with curiosity to know what she got me. What gift did she think of and why? Will it be meaningful? Will it be something silly - a joke of some kind?

How could I have forgotten about it?

Why didn't I open it on the night she gave it to me? I can't even remember why. I think I was overwhelmed. But I didn't open it which means I obviously never even said thank you to her for doing that for me.

I sigh, thick with regret again. I really am a fucking idiot.

I carry the black box back to my bed and sit on the edge, pulling the ribbon off and lifting the lid to peer inside.

Fuck.

This is a very well thought out gift.

This is super personalized.

A watch I have been wanting for ages, but it's pretty rare. Limited edition. Every time I tried to get one, they didn't have them available.

She got one for me.

I can't believe this.

I have to make it up to her. All the effort she put in that went unnoticed.

In the morning, I am up and dressed and waiting downstairs before Leora comes down. She is dressed and ready to go out, as she has been every day.

"This is for you." I say, handing her my black credit card. "There is no limit on the card."

It might not be the most personalized gesture, but it's a start.

CHAPTER EIGHTEEN
Leora

"Why are you giving me this?" I stare down at the black credit card. My father used to have one. I guess that was before all of his money issues. Even when he had one though - he would never have just handed it to me like this.

"I want you to go out and spoil yourself today. Have some fun." He smiles and I eye him through narrowed lids. What game is he playing now?

I bite at the inside of my cheek, wondering if it's a good idea for me to take this or not.

But then I smirk.

"Thanks." I say, sliding the card into the inside pocket of my handbag.

I clearly can't have an emotional relationship with him. My married life is doomed to be this lonely empty fake thing - but - I can take advantage of his money and at least get some joy out of this arrangement.

"What time will you be home?" He asks, standing too close to me.

I step back. "I won't be home for dinner." I say.

"You have to eat, Leora."

"I am meeting Isabelle for cocktails this afternoon and we'll get some pizza or something."

"Oh, ok, that sounds fun. Well, just message me so I know you're safe. Let me know if you need a ride home. I'll come and fetch you."

"I'll get the driver to take me." I raise one brow at him, so confused about what the fuck he's up to. Why is he trying to be nice?

I don't want to get roped into thinking he likes me again. I can't take that risk. I can't open my heart again - it will kill me if I am stupid enough to do that and he pushes me away.

It's not worth it.

He's made it clear - I remind myself.

"Alright, but if you change your mind and want me to fetch you - just call." He leans down and catches me by surprise when he kisses me goodbye. "Have fun, Leo." He grins.

"Leo?"

"Like a little wild kitten." He chuckles.

I pull the corner of my mouth to the side. Nicknames. He really is up to something.

I sigh and step away from him. "Alright. I'm going."

"Don't you want coffee? I can make you one to go?"

"No - thanks anyway. Have a good day."

He smiles, but it's a little less cheerful. I don't think he likes it when I say no to him.

Well, surprise asshole, you've earned all the no's I give you.

I go overboard.

I mean - ridiculous.

I buy everything I want and more. I am kind of horrified with myself about the amount of money I spent today - and I know that when I get home, he's going to be furious with me. I can't blame him. I just - I went too far. That's all.

I started shopping, and once I got going my mind sort of flipped into this mode where I wanted to get revenge on him for hurting me - *and* I was all in with the 'I can't have love, but I can have pretty things' justification.

The driver keeps carrying my shopping bags back to the car for me and I can even tell by the look on his face that I've gone too far.

Now I'm nervous to go home.

I giggle to myself as I swipe Masaccio's credit card again - paying for a pair of diamond earrings that I have to have. Even though I've spent too much - there is no point in stopping now. I'm already going to be in trouble. He'll take the card away the minute I get home, so I may as well get what I want now.

I was going to message Isabelle and invite her for cocktails. But at this point my feet are hurting, I'm too tired, and I want to go home and browse through all my new things. I can repack my closet and decorate my bedroom with the little cute things I got to make it feel more like home.

I glance at my watch.

I've been shopping for six hours. I stopped for a coffee and a little lunch, but that only took about forty minutes. That's just insane. I have never shopped for that many hours in one day before.

No wonder I'm so tired.

I can't even remember everything I bought, I realize with shock, then laugh at myself again.

Laugh now - cry later when Mas tears your head off.

I continue to grin. Whatever. This is his fault.

Slinging my new Versace handbag over my shoulder I shrug, I guess it's time to face the music at home.

I message the driver to meet me out front and then, swinging the last of my shopping items in their pretty paper bags, I walk towards the exit - and towards the inevitable lecture I am about to get. It'll still be worth it.

Arriving back home I feel a little tense.

The driver has to call one of the security guys to help carry all of my shopping bags up to my room and even together they have to do two trips.

I walk into the house with a nervous step - peeking around the corner - waiting for Mas to come marching towards me with a face of rage.

Nothing.

Silence.

If I'm quick, I can rush to my room and close the door and face his wrath another day.

I make a run for it, but he catches me at the top of the stairs.

"Leo - I thought you were going out for dinner."

"I - changed my mind." I say too.

"Ok, well join me then. You mentioned pizza this morning, and it made me crave it all day. I've ordered two. Do you like mushroom and salami?"

"I do." I eye him, waiting for the outburst. Did he not get notifications on his phone every time I swiped the card?

He reaches his arm out and wraps it around my waist, guiding me back downstairs.

As I walk, I step to the side, out of his reach.

I don't want him to touch me. I like it too much when he touches me, and I don't want to put my heart at risk like that.

Sleeping with him last night was a huge mistake that I want to avoid making again.

For him it's just sex - for me - it's too intimate. It provokes my feelings.

But my efforts to avoid him are useless because he just moves closer again and presses his hand against my lower back as he leads me to the kitchen.

Two pizza boxes are sitting on the kitchen counter. I move to lift the lid to peek at what he ordered. I hope there isn't any pineapple on here. Although - clearly, we aren't soulmates or anything, he *would* like pineapple.

I laugh at my thought.

Mas steps close to me and leans over to peek at the pizza too. Then in one movement too quick for me to escape - he wraps his hands around my hips and lifts me onto the kitchen counter. I sit there bewildered for a second, my feet hanging off the side.

"I think we can just eat in here. Do you want salt or that spicy sauce?"

"Um. Salt. Um - yes, the spicy sauce too."

He fetches both and opens the lids of both boxes - sitting them next to each other near me so I can pick which one I want.

He hands me the salt and I sprinkle some on top, while he splashes the chili sauce over both.

Then - to my horror he picks up a slice, leans against the counter between my legs - and offers me a bite.

I lean back so fast I knock my head on the cupboard behind me.

He chuckles. But thankfully he steps away.

"Here you go." He says, handing it to me from where he is now leaning against the counter next to me.

I take a deep breath, trying to focus on how good the pizza is.

He's being very touchy - very affectionate.

Is this his way of saying he wants sex again?

I want to distract him or change the subject.

So, I do something stupid and bring up the money I spent today, knowing it will put an end to him being so nice.

"Do you get notifications when I spend money on your card?" I ask, because he for whatever reason - doesn't get them or didn't check them yet.

"Yes. Why do you ask?"

"Oh. So, you checked them today." He can't have.

"Yes, I saw the notifications." He looks confused. And now I am confused.

"Oh."

"Why are you asking, Leo?"

"Um - because - *I spent a lot*." I blurt out.

He laughs. "Was that a lot?"

What the fuck? He isn't bothered at all.

I stop talking and start stuffing my face with pizza to prevent myself from asking more questions. My mind is chaotic with confused thoughts pushing in from all directions. He doesn't mind at all that I spent that much. He's being affectionate. He's being sweet and talking to me.

Suddenly I feel overwhelmed and terrified that I am going to start falling in love with him again - still - *fuck*.

"I'm full. Thanks for the pizza." I say quickly, sliding off the counter. I have to get away from him. This is so bad.

"Do you want something to drink?"

"Nope."

I run out of the kitchen before he can say another word.

I bolt up to my bedroom, closing the door, and leaning against it - shaking my head in disbelief.

CHAPTER NINETEEN
Masaccio

No matter what I do Leora is still acting cold and distant.

I need to make a bigger gesture. Something she can't ignore.

"Nathan." I call out as I walk towards the security room at the back of the house. I know he was reviewing the weeks footage and then writing his general report.

"Mas, I'm in here." His voice carries through to me.

I step into the room. He has two other guys working on the computers. It's a pretty boring job - reviewing camera footage. Not something I would ever want to do.

"Can I talk to you?"

"Of course." He stands up and follows me to the room filled with the blue glare from too many screens.

"I need you to organize something for me. It has to be a complete surprise. I don't want Leora knowing anything until it's ready."

"Ok." He says, tilting his head to the side and waiting.

"You know that guy who imports exotic cars? I saw a Chevrolet Corvette in his warehouse last week. I want it. Most likely he arranged it for another client, but I'll pay more than what he's asking. I also want it done in a custom color."

"I can go over there and see if he's willing to negotiate. I know he owes you a favor so we can call it in."

"Yes - do that."

I grin, knowing she is going to love this gift.

"What color do you want the car?"

"Fuchsia pink - with a glitter coat."

Nathan pulls a face. He doesn't even try to hide his distaste of my choice.

I laugh. "Obviously it's for Leora - not me."

"Yeah - that poor car, sir. It doesn't deserve to be put through that kind of torture."

I laugh again. I love his sense of humor.

"Well, I want to really grab her attention with this gift. So fuchsia it is."

"You'll be grabbing attention alright." He snorts a laugh. "Alright. I'll head over there now to chat to the guy. I'll let you know the outcome."

It takes three days for the car to be ready. Including the paint job which they do brilliantly. I head over to the warehouse to make sure it's up to my standards and I can't find a single thing wrong with it.

I nod, satisfied and the guy tosses me the keys. "It's all yours."

"Thanks. My girl is going to love it."

The engine growls as I rev it, then pull out of the warehouse and speed all the way home. Leora is out for the day, still avoiding me, still playing it cool when she is around me - but when she gets home, there is going to be something special waiting for her.

I park the Corvette right in front of the stairs leading to the front door, then wrap the giant black silk ribbon around the bonnet.

All that is left is to wait for her.

I'm not the most patient man in the world, so I hardly get anything done as I pace up and down the house continuously listening out for her.

Finally, just before sunset I hear the driver arriving and I hurry to greet her at the door.

I can't even hide the massive grin on my face as she climbs out of the car and her entire face looks shocked when she stares at the bright pink car waiting for her.

The driver pulls away to park the town car around the back and Leora is left alone on the driveway with her new Corvette.

I walk down the stairs towards her.

"Do you like it?" I am still grinning.

She looks from me to the car then back at me "What is this all about?" She asks.

"Just a little gift for my wife. Something fun, and beautiful - like you."

"Fun - and beautiful. I see."

She walks around the car slowly, tracing her finger over the smooth paint finish. I follow her, waiting for her reaction. I think she is a little shocked. Maybe overwhelmed by the gift.

"Do you want to take her for a spin?" I ask, pulling the driver's side door open. "You can take me for a sunset drive." I gesture for her to climb into the car.

"Actually, I think I am going to head upstairs to have a shower. It's been a long day. We can go for a drive another day."

My mouth drops open in disbelief. She doesn't look impressed in the smallest bit. She doesn't look excited or happy about the gift at all. She is just being her now normal cold and distant self.

I felt my jaw muscles clenching.

Leora is halfway up the stairs heading inside the house when she turns around and smiles.

"Thank you for the gift, Masaccio." She says formally.

I sigh as she turns away again. "It's a pleasure." I mutter under my breath, then stare down at the keys in my hand.

I guess, maybe she'll enjoy it once she takes it for a drive.

I leave the car parked there. If she goes out tomorrow, she can take it.

But I feel angry inside. Disappointed. Let down.

I know I said in the beginning that this was nothing but a marriage for show - but I've changed my mind now.

I want her.

She's my wife and I want a proper relationship with her.

She's beautiful and funny and sweet and warm and kind - when she isn't shutting me out - and I am desperate to go back to the way things were before I fucked it all up by being the coldest asshole on the planet.

"Dammit." I swear under my breath as I head inside too.

I guess there is only one thing left to do to make her see how much I feel for her now.

The next morning Leora heads out, to my relief she takes the Corvette. Thank fuck for that. And while she is out, I get all the house staff to work.

I am moving her entire bedroom into mine. She is my wife, and she will no longer be staying in a separate room from me.

This bullshit has been going on long enough, and it's time for us to be a proper couple. That means sharing a room and sleeping in the same bed.

To make sure she can't argue against this I also have the house staff put her bed in storage. Out of the way. So, there is nowhere else for her to sleep but in my bedroom.

This time I am not pacing when I wait for her to come home.

I'm relaxed, getting my work done, feeling less distracted because I know I've made the right choice.

When I hear her Corvette arriving home, I get up to greet her.

She walks into the house with a few items in her hands. I take them and set them on the entrance hall table then pull her against me to hug her. She stands stiff and awkward but doesn't push me away. "Hello, Leo. The chef was just about to start dinner. Have you got any requests?"

"No, he can go ahead with whatever he had planned."

Her voice is bland, empty, too calm. I want to shake her or slap her and bring back that bubbly beautiful girl who first moved in here after we got married.

I really miss her.

I want her back.

Leora waits for me to stop hugging her, as patient as ever, then steps away, picks up her things and heads upstairs - towards her room which isn't her room anymore.

I wait in the living room. Giving her the space to figure it out for herself.

From upstairs I hear an angry shout.

"What the hell is going on, Masaccio?"

She comes running down the stairs in a rage.

"Where are my things? What have you done with my clothes?"

"Everything has been moved over to my room. You and I will be sharing a bed from now on." I say, ignoring her outburst.

"Is this some kind of joke? Because it's not funny. Put everything back right now." She yells at me. But I look down at my phone and ignore her. I knew she wouldn't be happy about it at first, but she will adjust.

"My bed isn't even in the room anymore —I—I—" she stammers.

"Leo, it's going to be fine. We are husband and wife. My bed is very comfortable. All of your things are packed in your new cupboards. Everything is there."

She glares at me for the longest time. I stare back, my expression relaxed, soft even. She will come round. She has no choice.

CHAPTER TWENTY
Leora

I cannot believe the smug look on his face. As though he has me right where he wants me.

I don't understand what type of game he is playing with me right now. First pushing me away - then letting me spend way too much of his money as though it means nothing - then buying me a ridiculous fucking car, a beautiful car - and now moving my things into his bedroom. Why the hell would he do all of that? None of it makes sense.

It didn't make sense when he wasn't interested in me on our wedding night, and it makes little sense that he is now forcing me to share his bed whether or not I want to. He thinks the entire world revolves around what he wants when he wants it - with no regard for what I want.

Why does he want to taunt me with this kind of stuff anyway when he's made it clear we aren't in an actual relationship?

A relationship that is all for show.

Well, he is taking this 'for show' thing way too far. I guess that is what the car is all about. So that I can drive around town, and everyone can look at me and say, 'oh that's Masaccio's wife'.

I stand in the doorway of the living room glaring at him, but he looks calm and unaffected by my anger.

He *wants* to play games. He's enjoying this. Maybe I'm just some kind of toy to him he thinks he can mess with for fun. Is it possible that he is that sadistic?

I grit my teeth together, my hands clenched at my side and my shoulders feeling tight.

I won't be played with.

I won't be treated like this.

Without a word I spin on my heels and march back up to the bedroom - *our* bedroom - I flop down onto the bed, thinking, trying to figure out what to do.

I can't sleep in this room.

Everything smells like him. It's his space. It's all of his belongings.

I had just made my room feel like home. It was my little tranquil spot where I could just relax and be me without worrying what he was thinking of me or if I was annoying him. Because I always felt like I was annoying him.

I do note that a few of my decor pieces have been set up here and there, but they look out of place and as uncomfortable as I feel in this male dominated room. Even the vase of flowers and the monstera plant near the window - they don't belong in this room. The energy is all wrong.

I grab my phone from my handbag and open my browser.

I have an idea. I need to do some research - and then when he is asleep tonight, I'll carry out my plan.

And the bottom line is - fuck him for forcing me into this situation and giving me no other choice.

Once I've gathered all the information, I need I put my phone down on the bedside table, I climb off the bed and grab my travel case from the closet - I take a moment to find it. Pausing for a second to listen - trying to figure out where in the house he is. But I hear nothing. I better move quickly.

I throw clothes into it. I'm not paying attention to what I'm packing but I also calm myself knowing that if I forget something I can just get it there. I have to pack and then hide the bag, so he doesn't see it. I keep stopping to listen. Pausing just long enough to make sure he isn't coming up the stairs, then refocusing on my task.

When the bag is packed, with my clothes, toiletries, and passport, I tuck it into the back of my closet.

My heart is racing when I climb into bed in my black tracksuit, I'm dressed and ready to go as soon as he is asleep. It's a waiting game now so I pull the covered over my head. I'll pretend to be asleep until he falls asleep - then I'll make my getaway.

I can't believe I am going to do it - but I'm going to the airport, I'll buy a ticket to Hawaii when I get there. I think I just need to get away for a bit. I don't need him knowing either because I'm sure he will try to stop me.

I feel terrible for doing this behind his back, but he's left me no choice.

A week should be enough time to get my thoughts together.

I guess I can see how it goes and stay longer if I need to. The time away from him should hopefully give me the clarity I need to figure out what I want to do with my life and how I can get through this horrible situation and stay sane.

Masaccio comes to bed late, and goes through a slow, relaxed process of getting ready for bed. He pays me very little attention as I continue to pretend to be asleep.

My heart is beating faster by the minute. I just want him to fall asleep, dammit.

When he does, I feel dizzy with nerves. I move as quickly, but as quietly as I can to grab my travel bag from the closet and head downstairs without making a sound.

I feel like a bit of an asshole as I sneak out of the front door.

On the steps in the front of the house I pull my sneakers on. I told the Uber driver to wait for me just outside the property.

As long as I am on the plane before he checks the notifications that I booked a ticket.

All the way to the airport I have my eyes continuously checking the rearview mirror, but there is no sign of him. He is still asleep, I hope. Completely unaware that I'm not lying next to him.

At the airport I hurry to the counter and book a ticket, I'm really lucky before the next flight is boarding in thirty minutes and I made it just in time to be on it.

Sitting on the plane, staring out of the window next to me at the land far below - a beautiful view with the city lights flickering like stars on the ground - I feel immense guilt. It's not like me at all - to just up and leave without telling anyone. I also feel relieved though because I'm on my way. Mas didn't arrive out of nowhere or send some of his men to stop me just as I was boarding.

I made it.

I'm getting away for a little while.

I need this more than I think I know.

Ever since the wedding I was in a little bit of a dream land. It all happened so fast, and I've changed so much since then. I guess I've grown up a lot - a dose of pain and the harsh slap of reality will do that to a person.

Leaning my head back I close my eyes. I'm too anxious to sleep, but I should at least try.

Arriving in Hawaii I forget all my concerns. The energetic, bubbly and viby nature of this place wakes me up and has me excited for this time alone.

I ask the taxi driver to take me to the beach near where we stayed last time. Once I am there, I find a little beach chalet - something small, just for me - and I book it for a week.

That will be enough time to sort my head out, clear my thoughts and get away from Mas so that I can figure it all out.

Standing on the front deck looking towards the ocean I am smiling, but my heart feels heavy.

I wish things had gone differently. I wish this place, where I had my honeymoon, was filled with fond memories instead of memories of being rejected repeatedly.

I'll have to make fresh memories here - on my own - diving, hiking, making new friends.

I sit out on the deck watching the sun sink into the ocean.

I try not to think about him.

But in truth - he is all I can think about.

CHAPTER TWENTY-ONE
Masaccio

I stretch my legs out and feel the pull of sleepy muscles. I slept really well.

A deep sleep with pleasant dreams.

Rolling over towards Leora's side of the bed I run my hand over the sheet, searching for her. But she's not there and the blankets are cold where she would have been lying.

I guess she got up early.

I wonder if she slept well. I know I was very pushy moving her things in here, but I just want her near me, and she keeps blocking me. This was the only way I could think for her to be close to be without being able to run away.

I toss the blankets aside and sit up, stretching my arms and back, yawning. Then I climb out of bed and head downstairs where I can hopefully have a coffee with my wife and maybe talk to her a little about the changes I made.

But she's not in the kitchen.

I make a cup coffee for each of us anyway, then carry hers through to the living room - the outside patio - the pool area.

Finally, I spot Nathan walking around the garden.

"Nathan, have you seen Leora this morning?"

"No, sir. Not yet. I thought she was still sleeping."

I shake my head. "No, she wasn't in bed when I woke up this morning."

"Her car is still out front." He says, referring to the pinkest car on the planet.

"Ok, well she has to be around here somewhere." I shrug, heading back inside.

But my search through the house turns up nothing and soon I start to feel a nauseous tension building in the pit of my stomach.

Where the hell is she?

I dial her phone, but it goes straight to voicemail.

Shit.

Well, she's definitely not here. There is only one way in and out of this property and the camera would have seen her.

I head to the security room, telling Nathan to meet me there.

We got through the footage from the night before and my heart shatters when I see it.

She is carrying a suitcase out of the main gate and getting into a waiting car outside of the property.

Nathan remains quiet as we watch it - then I tell him to rewind and play it again - and again.

I can't believe it.

She left.

She left me.

She didn't ask for a divorce, but I imagine the request will be coming soon. It's unheard of to divorce from an arranged marriage after such a short time - but she left.

Was I really that terrible?

So terrible that she couldn't even bear the thought of living with me anymore?

Maybe I need to get a team together to look for her. Just bring her back home and work this out.

I pull my phone out of my pocket again, ignoring all the notifications at the top because I am focused on only one thing - finding out where my wife went.

While I am busy figuring out what to do next an idea sparks.

She still has my card.

Even the Uber would have been booked on it. I can then find out where she went.

I pull all the notifications down, searching for anything that mentions an amount spent on the card I gave her.

My head spins when I see it.

She bought a ticket to Hawaii.

She's not even in the same city as me anymore. She's out of my time zone - on a different part of the planet.

Did she go there with someone else?

Is that what she has been doing these past few weeks - meeting with someone new - cheating on me? And now she is meeting them in Hawaii for a romantic getaway?

Would she really be that cold?

Was I that much of an asshole that I pushed her that far?

Was I?

I slump down onto the chair near to me in front of the rows of monitors that are used to survey my property. My entire body feels limp and useless. My heart is pulling so tight in my chest I wonder if this is what a heart attack feels like. But I know it's just pain. Emotional pain.

Because I can't lie and tell myself I *wasn't* that cruel.

I was.

I was a complete dickhead.

I was nasty and cold, and I pushed her away so effectively that it worked.

I achieved what I was planning on achieving - except by the time it worked I wanted something different. I want her. I want my wife.

"Sir? Masaccio?" Nathan sounds worried as he leans closer to me. He reaches out and grabs my shoulder, squeezing hard. "Masaccio. Are you ok?"

"Um - yeah. I'm - she went to Hawaii. She flew there last night." I say, void of emotion.

"Oh." Nathan says, looking unsure of what it all means.

I shake my head. "I need to be alone." I say, standing up and leaving the security room.

I head into our bedroom. Stripping my sweatpants and T-shirt off I get into the shower. I need to think clearly, and a cold shower will help me do that.

Is there any chance of winning her back at this point?

I doubt it. If she has already met someone else - I really fucked up.

She was so into me when we first got together and for some reason that I don't even understand I couldn't even try to love her back.

I couldn't even try to let her close to me.

I am a terrible person.

A monster of sorts.

My father was right about me - I have one purpose in life and that is to run the family business. I am not good for anything else.

I was not made to be loved - or to feel love.

The cold-water stings over my skin and creates a wave of goosebumps. I force myself to stand there, feeling the bite of the cold.

The best thing I can do for her at this point, and for myself, is to just let her do whatever she wants to.

I've already done enough damage. And I know I hurt her. That's why she became so distant and off towards me.

I have hurt her enough to drive her into the arms of another man and now I am the one who is suffering.

It is the consequences of my own actions.

And I have to live with them.

There is nothing I can do at this point. I have ruined my chances with her, and she is the only woman I have ever felt anything for in this way.

When I climb out of the shower I am shivering.

The ache in my body helps distract me from the ache in my heart.

I hear Dalila's voice from downstairs, chatting to Nathan.

I get dressed and head down towards the noise.

"Mas, oh wow, you look like you didn't sleep at all. What's wrong?"

"I slept just fine."

Nathan takes his cue and leaves the kitchen.

"Ok, then what's going on? You look like shit." She says, sliding onto the counter as I turn the coffee machine on for my second coffee of the day.

"I don't want to talk about it." I answer.

"Ugh. Why do you have to be so annoying? You know you being this closed off is the reason your wife is struggling to get closed to you." She rolls her eyes. "Where is Leora? I came to see if she wants to go shopping with me today."

"My wife left me, Dalila. Because I am cold and distant and cruel. She left."

Dalila is staring at me with her mouth dropped open and her eyes as wide as I have ever seen them. "No way." She mutters. "Leora was so into you. There is no way she left. We can go fetch her right now. I am sure this is just a misunderstanding."

"There is no misunderstanding. She is in Hawaii. She snuck out last night. Caught a taxi to the airport and left." I shrug, trying to be calm about it despite the ache in my heart.

"So, go fucking get her."

I shake my head.

"I can't. I have destroyed all my chances with her. She won't take me back."

CHAPTER TWENTY-TWO
Leora

Hawaii is such a beautiful place. And I am doing my best to stay busy every day. I've been on two diving lessons, and a sunset trip to the reef. But I feel empty and lonely.

The hotel staff are really sweet, and the other guests are friendly.

I've made a few friends, but I am sort of keeping to myself because I need to think.

Have another diving lesson after breakfast today. I'm not even hungry.

I should eat - but instead I am walking along the beach.

The sand feels good between my toes. It's warm and soft. I stay near the edge of the water and when the waves splash up onto the shore they wrap around my ankles and caress me.

"Leora." I hear a cheerful voice call my name from a little way behind me.

I turn to see Daniel running up towards me.

"Hey, Dan. How are you this morning?" I smile.

I met him on my second night here. He's here for his brother's wedding and we were at the bar having sundowners at the same time. He's really sweet. Very flirty. But I don't flirt back. I'm here to clear my head, not to make things more complicated.

Having a friend to talk to is nice though.

"I was calling you for a while." He chuckles as he reaches me.

"Sorry, deep in thought over here."

"Yeah, this place does that to you. It's so beautiful. Listen - I took your advice and I'm going for a diving lesson this morning. There is a group going out with Tony at eleven—"

"Oh, I'm part of that group." I point to them with a laugh.

"Really? Are you serious? Well, I guess that makes this my lucky day doesn't it."

I grin up at him as he stands there watching me. His eyes are bright and happy. His entire aura is relaxed and welcoming.

He's an awesome guy. In another life I guess I could have fallen for someone like him. Tall, dark hair, dark brown eyes - a damn fine build -

But not in this life.

In this life I got cursed. I got to fall in love with *and marry* a man doesn't want me.

"Well, then I guess I will see you there. It's my third lesson. Tony is an excellent teacher. I was nervous at first, but he makes it easy."

"Awesome. Ok. I'll leave you to the rest of your walk. See you later beautiful girl."

"See you later Dan."

He makes my heart feel happy. But not in that love kind of way.

I turn my attention back to the sand, the sun and the bright blue sky scattered with white clouds.

As I walk, I compare Masaccio to Daniel. There is no competition. My heart, as stupid as it is, is with Masaccio. Whether I like it or not.

He's just - he's -

I sigh.

I need to let it go. Dammit.

I'm just hurting myself.

By the time I get back home I have to be in a different frame of mind. One where I don't mind if he doesn't care about me. One where I can live in the same house as him and not be tormented day in and day out by my stupid emotions.

I walk a little further along the beach and then turn back.

I'll just enjoy my dive this morning and figure it out as I go along.

I have another four days in paradise. Then it's back to my life - whatever that means.

The crystal-clear ocean water splashes against the side of the boat.

Dan and his friend from the wedding group and laughing and joking as they sort out their goggles and diving gear.

We don't need wetsuits as it's not cold enough, and we are diving with small handheld tanks because it's just a beginner's course.

I pull my goggles down over my face and sit on the edge of the boat, ready to jump in.

Tony shouts. "Every one ready?" Then without waiting for our reply he leaps off the boat and splashes into the water.

I jump in straight away.

I love this. I never knew I could feel this connected to the ocean. The salt seems to soak into my skin and improve my mood the second I submerge.

It's a different world under the water. One where I can escape the heart ache of love.

Daniel swims over to me, always with that massive smile on his face.

We've been diving for about thirty minutes so far.

He's a natural.

"This is incredible. Thanks so much for recommending it." He says, lifting his goggles to wipe the fog off the inside.

"I know. I think I am going to dive every day until I leave."

"Well, I'd love to join—"

"Shark." Someone in the group screams.

Tony already warned us the reef sharks might make an appearance. I was really horrified when he said that, but he assured us repeatedly that all we have to do is stay calm.

That person scream - is not calm.

Dan swims closer to me and wraps his arm around my waist.

"Don't worry. I'll stay with you. Let's head back to the boat."

For a second, I'm frozen.

Fear gripping every cell in my body. But Tony's reassurance loops in my head.

I shake my head. "I don't want to get out." I grin.

Dan looks at me as though I've lost my mind. I take a deep breath and dive under, swimming towards Tony and the rest of the group, looking for the shark.

The first shark I see is a young reef shark. Only about a meter long. And it is magnificent.

Yes, it's terrifying. Just the idea of being in the water with a shark is terrifying. But the longer I stay and watch it - the more beautiful it becomes.

And there isn't just one. There are about six of them.

I do as Tony instructs. I don't kick or splash too much and if it swims near me, I remain controlled, facing it.

And I love every second of this dive.

By the time we are back on the boat I realize that this is the experience that shows me my true strength. The fact that I can be brave and strong and stay in control of my emotions no matter what happens.

After my week in Hawaii is over and I have to go home to Masaccio - I will treat him like that shark.

Beautiful and dangerous - something incredible to look at - but not something I should turn my back on. Or let my guard down around. I won't kick or splash or draw attention to myself, but I will be watching and cautious at all times, that is how I will keep my heart safe.

I cannot allow myself to fall in love with him again. Or admit to it and let my heart feel it.

I will treat him like that shark, and I will stay in control around him.

That night, still on an adrenalin high from our experience with the sharks, the entire dive team meets at the local beach bar for cocktails and sundowners.

We are dancing and having fun, but my heart is still heavy. I do my best to push it aside. I hate the fact that I miss him.

I hate the fact that even in such a beautiful place I can't stop thinking about him.

But it is what it is, and I will get over it.

Daniel grabs my arm and pulls me to the dance floor. I follow him, already thinking of excuses to leave.

I don't really want to dance, but I notice the rest of my friends from the dive this morning are dancing, so I follow him and make sure to stand with everyone - not just him.

I should allow myself time to relax and make the most of this holiday. This experience is about me finding myself and healing my heart. That's what I came here for and that is all that matters.

All of us are chatting and enjoying the music and Daniel is being flirty, but not overly annoying about it. I just play it cool and polite with him.

CHAPTER TWENTY-THREE
Masaccio

"So, go fucking get her."

I shake my head.

"I can't. I have destroyed all my chances with her. She won't take me back."

My sister throws me a death glare. "Don't be stupid." She snaps at me, sliding off the kitchen counter. "That girl really liked you a lot Masaccio. Whatever you did to make her leave - you can still fix it by just going after her."

"Not if she is there with someone else." I snarl back at her. Getting angry because she won't drop this subject, and I don't want to talk about it because it's upsetting me too much.

"What in the world makes you think she is there with someone else?"

"Why else would she go to Hawaii?"

"Um - because it's where you had your honeymoon. Jeez Mas, all you need to do is try. There is nothing that can go wrong if you just try. If you *don't try*, you *will* lose her though."

I blink at my sister. The truth of her words has shocked me into silence. If I do nothing - then I really one hundred percent have lost Leora, and I will never be able to forgive myself. She's right. She's so fucking right.

"I have to go to Hawaii." I say, a whisper.

"Yes, you do."

"Call the pilot. Book a flight for as soon as possible. I need to grab a bag." I bolt upstairs while Dalila sorts out my flight for me, getting the pilot to meet me at the runway near my private jet.

I grab my car keys and rush towards the front door. Pausing, just for a second, to give my sister a quick hug and kiss on the cheek.

"Thanks, Lila. I - just *thanks*."

She grins and pushes me away. "Hurry up. Go get your girl back." She laughs, then watches me bolt out the door.

I arrive at the airport feeling anxious. All this time I've wasted sulking at home. All this time I could have already been there with her. Well, there is no point in stressing about the things I can't change at this point. What I need to focus on is what I can change - and how I am going to win her back.

I've showered her in gifts, I've given her material things - but the one thing I haven't done is told her how I feel. I guess I didn't understand or know I how felt until she was already gone. But I owe her that.

I have to do this right because I think I only have one more chance - if I even have that.

On the flight I do my best to get some sleep. I am going to arrive in Hawaii after sunset.

I know which villa she booked into because I saw the statements on the credit card. I know where to go. Everything is going to be fine.

The lady at reception points me towards the beach.

"Leora is over there, at the beach bar where the music is." She smiles. "Oh, so you know her?" I ask, surprised she didn't even have to look up the room number or anything.

"Everyone knows her - and everyone loves her. She's amazing." She replies as though I should already know this.

I do.

I know how amazing she is.

"Thanks." I say, turning towards the beach.

The music is loud, and people are laughing and talking over it. They are clearly having the best time.

I stand to the side, near the bar, scanning the crowd trying to find her. It doesn't take me long to spot her. She radiates beauty and catches my attention within moments.

But as soon as I find her - I see the man who is all over her on the dance floor.

Is that who she left me for?

She is wearing a soft, flowing summer dress that moves around her body in elegant waves like water.

It looks incredible on her. She looks beautiful, like she belongs in paradise.

Her hair is pinned up in a high and messy bun. It looks like it's been touched by seawater. A little wild.

The man laughs at something she said.

Jealousy surges like acid inside me. I want to tear him apart.

I want to walk straight up to them and smash my fist into his face and not stop until he's choking on his own blood.

I grit my teeth, clenching my jaw until the muscles hurt.

I can't seem to move. I'm just bolted to this spot, watching them.

But the longer I watch the more it seems that my first impression was wrong.

She is chatting to the guy, they are dancing together - and from his side - sure as shit he is doing his best to flirt with her - but she is keeping him at a distance. She is trying to share her attention amongst her other friends she is dancing with. She's talking to everyone.

The guy moves closer to her again and places his hand on her waist, pulling her around to face him and every nerve ending in my body catches on fire as I get ready to walk over there and rip him to pieces.

But I don't have to.

Because as he leans close to her - she places her hand on his chest and pushes him away, shaking her head. I can see she is being nice about it - polite - and I can tell, even from here, that her rejection hurt him.

She has turned him down.

Relief washes through me. She turned him down. So, she wasn't with him. She wasn't here to have some fun with another guy.

The guy nods a few times, smiles, and then walks towards the bar. He looks up at me with disappointment in his eyes.

He leans against the bar, orders a beer and then turns towards me.

"That didn't work out as I had hoped." He chuckles, his eyes void of the laughter spilling from his mouth.

"I guess you can't win them all." I reply.

"Yeah - but she is something special man. I mean, I have only spoken to her a few times - but sometimes you just know when you've found a really special one."

His eyes fall and he stare down at his beer. "Anyway." He sighs and turns his back on me.

I don't go to Leora straight away. For some reason I am happy to just watch her for now. I think it is because this is the space between hoping that I can still make this work for her - and having a definitive answer. Somehow not having the answer - not being turned down - is easier for now.

But at some point, I will have to face this.

I drink my beer and watch as she dances with some people she knows, laughing a little, but not looking entirely like herself. There is a spark missing. A glitter in her eyes that was there when we first got married - before I hurt her.

It is my responsibility to make her smile again. Her real smile.

The one I stole from her.

Leora turns and looks towards the bar. It's like she is moving in slow motion.

Her dress floats around her body. My eyes are on her as she looks up and at me.

She freezes. I can see a look of panic in her eyes. But very quickly, so quickly I might even think I misread it, the look is replaced by defiance. A certain resilience.

She stares at me with confidence. Her eyes narrowed and serious.

I tilt my head to the side and one corner of my mouth curls up into a smile.

Surprise. I think to myself with a laugh.

She looks surprised. That's for sure.

Leora sighs and tilts her head back. Then she walks towards me, her hips moving in ways that make it impossible for me to look anywhere else but at her.

"Leora." I say, with a smile, when she reaches me. She ignores me, leaning against the bar. The barman comes straight over to her. "What can I get you Leora." He asks.

"A gin for me and - whatever he's having - um - another beer."

Before she turns to give me her attention, I watch her face. She closes her eyes and takes a moment, looking as though she is gathering her thoughts.

CHAPTER TWENTY-FOUR
Leora

Daniel just tried to kiss me. His hand on my waist, he pulled me towards him and then tried to make his move. I guess I knew it was coming, but I am still a little shocked.

I feel terrible, because I know what it's like to be rejected.

But I am not interested in him, and I won't lead him to think I am.

I press my hand against his chest and as kindly as I can I say. "I'm sorry Daniel, but I'm not interested in you like that. I'm married. I'm sorry if I gave you the wrong impression."

"Oh." He stammers. "I didn't see a wedding ring. I just thought - uh - ya no problem. I'll - um - go get a beer." He steps backwards, bumping into one of the other people. Then he laughs uncomfortably and turns away from me.

I don't watch him. I immediately turn to the other people in our group. He must be feeling pretty horrible, and it won't help if I just keep staring at him.

I know he's gone towards the bar, and I want another drink, but I'd rather wait till he's moved on. In the meantime, I can just keep dancing and chatting to everyone here.

I sigh, my heart feels so heavy.

I really wish Masaccio was here. But not. Because the real Masaccio is not who I thought he was and the one I dreamed up in my head doesn't exist.

The one I dreamed up - he wants me. He was excited to marry me. The real one is cold and distant.

Finally, I can't handle the music anymore. I know my mood will bring everyone else down even though I am faking having a good time, I feel heart broken. The few drinks I've had aren't lifting me up they are making me feel more lost than ever.

I turn towards the bar, thinking maybe I'll have one more and -

My heart stops. My body freezes.

Am I seeing things?

That - no it can't be.

Masaccio.

Sitting at the bar with a smirk on his face as he stares at me.

Is it really him?

My heart is beating so fast the blood is pumping in my ears and I can't even hear the music at this point.

I take a deep breath. Close my eyes and tilt my head back.

I know why he's here.

It's not like he rushed to Hawaii to save our marriage. No. He's probably just pissed off that I used his credit card for my little escape - and maybe that I didn't even tell him where I was going.

His ego is most likely bruised because his wife isn't being obedient.

Well.

There is only one thing I can do.

I have to go there - and talk to him.

I gather up all my strength and courage and make my way towards him.

"Leora." He smiles at me. Looking relaxed.

But I will not make this easy for him.

I lean up against the bar. Waving Patrick over.

"What can I get you Leora." He asks.

"A gin for me and - whatever he's having - um - another beer."

Then, I take another breath, centering myself, before I turn to face him.

"Masaccio." I say his name.

"Leora." He says my name and my heart flips wildly. Why does it still do that?

Why does he still have the power to make me feel that way?

"What are you doing here, Mas?" I ask, deciding to get straight to the point.

"It's Hawaii, people come here to relax and have a good time, right?" he says, laughing. A deep sound that resonates through my body.

"They do - yes - do you even know how to have a good time?" I say sarcastically, remembering how boring he was on our honeymoon.

He waves Patrick over to us again.

"Two tequilas' please."

Patrick glances at me, trying to gauge if this tall dark stranger is bothering me or not. I nod, I need a tequila.

Masaccio lifts his shot and holds it out towards me. "To relaxing and having a good time."

"Ok." I say, skeptically.

He downs it, then orders another one for each of us. Mm. What is he up to?

Mas leans against the bar, reaching and tracing his hand over my hip.

"This dress looks incredible on you."

"Thanks."

I'm a little tipsy and he is starting to work his way through my defenses.

But I'm in Hawaii - and all this time I kept wishing he was here - and now he is and he's being sweet and fun.

We chat for a little while and it feels like he is meeting me for the first time. He's soft, funny, spontaneous.

He takes my hand and leads me towards the dance floor.

He pulls me up against his chest and I let out a little moan when I feel his body against mine. He feels so good.

The drinks are making my head spin a little. They are messing with my ability to maintain control.

He's too sexy. He's acting so differently. And this is the Mas that I wanted all along.

He slips his hand up my back, his fingers leaving a trail of fire on my skin.

His fingers thread through my hair and he pulls my head back, without warning - he presses his lips against mine. My heart slams against my ribs.

Fuck.

It feels so good.

I wrap my arms tighter around his waist, deepening the kiss.

A low growl rumbles from his chest, vibrating against me.

"Where is your villa, Leo?" He asks, and I know exactly what he wants. He wants what I want at this point, and I don't even care to stop him.

I step back, taking his hand, I lead him down the beach to my little villa.

As soon as we are through the door, he lifts me in his arms and carries me towards the bed. My legs are wrapped around his waist and his hands are pushing my skirt up my legs.

I am so desperate to feel him. All I've wanted is for him to want me - all this time.

He drops me onto the bed and stands over me, looking down at me with a wild look in his eyes.

"Untie the cord from your dress." He demands.

I sit up and pull the cord around my waist loose. He is unbuttoning his shirt when I pull my dress up over my head, tossing the cord to the side.

But he grins. Leaning down to pick it up, he pulls it through his hands.

Then he grabs my ankles and yanks me to the edge of the bed.

I let out a small scream - shocked by his aggressive move.

"Take your bikini off. I want to see all of you."

I wiggle out of my bikini, feeling my nipples grow hard and heat building between my legs. I can see the bulge of his cock pressing against his pants.

Fuck. I want him so badly.

"Hold out your wrists." His voice is deep, controlling me.

When I lift my wrists towards him, he grabs them both in one hand, then wraps the cord of my dress around them. Over and over again, before tying it securely.

I can't move my hands. He leans over the bed and wrapping his arm around my waist he lifts me higher onto it. Before I realize what, he is doing, he has my hands up against the ornate bars of the headboard - tying me to that.

"Mas." I let out a breathless whisper of his name.

He pulls my head to the side and kisses my neck sending shivers bolting through my body.

"Oh — fuck." I gasp.

His hand runs over my breasts, tweaking my nipples, pulling them gently. Then he wraps his mouth over my nipple and lets his tongue play over my sensitive skin.

I rock my hips up against him. I want to touch him.

Wiggling against the restraints they bite harder into my skin.

He grabs my thighs and pulls them apart, dipping his fingers inside me and I want to scream it feels so good.

He chuckles. It's a deep rumble that taunts me.

Pulling his pants open with one hand he frees his cock.

I can't take my eyes off it. The veins popping along the shaft. The size of it. I know how good he feels inside me.

I rock my hips up again.

"How badly do you want me to fuck you?" he asks, and my entire body feels alive with tension.

"Badly. Please." I beg.

He leans over me, spreading my legs as wide as they will go.

He pushes his cock up against my pussy and rocks his hips forward - sliding into me - inch by inch as I try to catch my breath.

Then he fucks me. I grab the headboard, desperate to hold on to something. I want to tear my nails down his back.

I scream his name, and it only seems to drive him harder into me.

Each thrust jolts my body as he slams into me.

I can feel the pleasure building, becoming too much, overwhelming me.

The orgasm slams into me and my entire body shudders.

He growls as he thrusts deep inside me, exploding his own pleasure as my pussy clamps over his cock.

CHAPTER TWENTY-FIVE
Masaccio

She is still tied to the bed. I lie next to her catching my breath. Her skin is shining with a thin layer of perspiration, and she has the most gorgeous grin on her face.

I roll towards her, reaching for the cord and pulling it loose.

She lowers her arms and rotates her wrists, rubbing them a little.

"Was it too tight?" I ask, concerned that I hurt her.

"Not at all." She says with a slight blush on her cheeks.

I grab her around the waist and pull her up against my body. It feels so good to just be here with her, to feel her skin against mine. Tonight, out at the beach bar - it was so much fun.

I want to tell her how I feel - that I'm sorry for the stupid way I acted. I want to explain to her I've never felt this way before and I'm not very good with words. But, I just stare at her instead, appreciating the soft curve of her cheek bones and the sharp dip of her collar bone.

I trace my fingers over it, following the shape of her body.

Her stomach growls loudly and she giggles.

"Are you hungry?" I ask, sitting up. "I can order some room service." I climb off the bed ready to find the hotel phone.

"Actually. I have a nice selection of leftovers in the fridge. I'm happy to snack on that."

"Alright. I can do with leftovers." I head towards the little kitchen and unpack three boxes from the fridge.

Roast chicken pieces, a stir-fry and some sushi. An interesting mix of assorted flavors.

SOMETHING OLD

Putting them all onto a plate, arranging them nicely, I carry it back towards the bed and sit down next to her.

She's pulled her floral dress back on, much to my disappointment.

"I don't know why you put this back on when I am just going to take it off again later." I grin, reaching out to touch her dress.

She leans up against the back of the bed, crossing her legs and pulling the plate of food towards herself.

She looks so relaxed. Content and happy. I wish I could see her like this all the time.

I can.

If I just open up to her and be honest about everything.

When we are done eating, I'll tell her.

Watching her I know it's real. I know without a doubt that I have fallen for her.

It seems like the universe was on my side this entire time - I just wasn't paying attention.

But it also seems that it's not too late.

I still have a chance. She is still willing to let me close to her.

She is chatting, telling me about her diving lessons and how she swam with sharks.

It's so good to hear her talking like this again.

I get nervous as the food finishes.

How am I going to word this? What am I going to say?

My jaw is clenching and unclenching, and I feel tension creeping into my shoulders.

Leora notices it too.

She stops talking and looks towards me.

"Is something wrong? Was I talking too much? Was I - was I annoying you?" She asks, sounding hurt.

"No - definitely not. Not at all - it's - I need to talk to you—"

"Ok." She sits up straighter, biting her lower lip.

"Leora, I know why you left. Uh - let me start from the beginning." I swallow hard. The beginning. Where is that? The kiss?

"Ever since this whole thing started - it happened really quickly. You have to understand that I have never seen myself as the type of guy who was going to get married. And then it was thrown at me. And then you stopped talking to me. And you just left. You didn't say a word. You snuck off in the middle of the night. Taking your bags. I saw you on the security cameras and I thought - she didn't even have the heart to tell me to my face that she was leaving. I was angry and hurt—"

Leora pushes herself off the bed and turns to glare at me. "Are you serious right now? You want to lecture me for leaving? You came all this way to get laid and then tell me I hurt your feelings by leaving? This has to be some kind of fucked up joke?" She yells at me.

Shit.

None of my words came out right. I wanted to tell her it hurt me when she left because I realized I have fallen for her. What did I say? Whatever I said has made her furious.

"Wait. Just listen to me." I say, standing up.

She grabs her cardigan and slides her arms into it.

"Actually, I don't have to listen to you for another second. I am so over you and the way you treat me. I don't deserve this. You are the biggest asshole I have ever met. I wish I had never met you. I can't believe I am stuck - married to you—" her words are clipped, angry, heated. She spits them at me with hurt in her voice. Her chest is heaving up and down as she huffs.

"Leora." I try again, but she pushes past me, towards the door, walking out of it and slamming it behind herself.

Fuck. That was terrible.

Why am I so fucking bad at this?

"Shit." I swear loudly. "I need to fix this - again." Searching around the room I find my shirt, pulling it on and rushing to do up the buttons.

I need to go find her.

It's a toss-up between giving her the space to calm down - or finding her and explaining that I didn't mean for it to sound like it did.

I push the door of the villa open and step out onto the sand.

Really there is no toss up at all. I have to find her and fix this.

It's dark, but the pathway on either side of the villa is lit with fairy lights - and above me the moon is bright, and the stars are glittering everywhere. It's a beautiful night. The kind of night where you hold someone special and tell them you love them.

I glance left, then right, trying to figure out which way she would have gone.

In the distance the party is still going at the beach bar. I can hear the music and laughter.

She would have wanted to be alone I imagine.

So, I turn in the opposite direction and walk along the beach - looking for her.

CHAPTER TWENTY-SIX
Leora

I stare at him in disbelief.

Did he really just say that to me?

Is he sitting there lecturing me on how I hurt him? I can't believe I was stupid enough to think he was any different from the person he has proven himself to be.

And I actually fell for it - all the gentleness - the niceness - the soft looks he was giving me and the way he touched me - *fuck*. I scream in my mind. I scream and curse myself because I feel so stupid. I feel like such a fucking idiot for dropping my guard.

This time - I can't even be angry with him - this time it was my fault. I knew better.

I made a mistake.

This one is on me.

He is who he is, and I fell for it again.

But of course, knowing all of that doesn't make it hurt any less.

I did, genuinely, open my heart up to him again.

I feel my chest caving in. My heart is breaking all over again.

Then the pain turns to a blazing rage of hurt.

I hate him.

I hate the fact that I had to marry him.

I hate that this is my life.

"Wait. Just listen to me." He says, as I push my arms into my cardigan, ready to run away from him - away from the hurt - away from my stupidity.

I spin towards him.

"Actually, I don't have to listen to you for another second. I am so over you and the way you treat me. I don't deserve this. You are the biggest asshole I have ever met. I wish I had never met you. I can't believe I am stuck - married to you." I'm being nasty. I hate he brings this person out of me. This isn't me. I shake my head to try to change my thoughts.

I need to leave.

"Leora." He calls my name again as I push the door open and step out into the cool night air.

My skin was kissed by the sun today. It's rosy and warm and even though it isn't too cold tonight, it's chilly against my skin.

I wrap my cardigan tighter around my chest.

Maybe it's not the cold that's biting at me.

Maybe it's his words. His cruelty.

I look towards the party at the beach bar. There are so many people there.

I could just blend into the crowd, keep drinking, hope for oblivion. But I am not that person either. And I can't face other people right now. So, I turn the other way and step off the path as I head towards the water line. There are too many lights on the path.

I want to hide away.

I want to be alone.

I can feel the ache in my chest growing the further I get from Masaccio.

At least any doubt I had is now gone.

I dared to hope, I dared to try again - at least I can't be blamed for not trying.

Tears stream down my cheeks as I walk, and it blurs my vision until I can barely see where I'm stepping.

So, I sit down.

I flop into the soft sand, pull my legs right up against my chest and hug my arms around them.

Looking out across the dark ocean and the most beautiful night sky everything in me breaks apart.

The tears flow stronger and loud sobs choke from my throat. I try to hold them back, but it's impossible.

Thank goodness I am not near anyone.

I bury my face against my arm and let myself cry. It's better to let it out, anyway.

I'm tired of trying to hold it together.

I'm over feeling like shit.

All I wanted was for my husband to love me.

My throat is hurting, dry and tight from crying so much.

"Leora."

I jump out of my skin when he says my name. I was so lost in my own emotions I didn't hear him walking towards me.

"What?" I snap. "Can't you just leave me alone?"

He sits down next to me and tries to wrap his arm around me.

"Stop that. Stop everything. Seriously. *Just leave me alone.*"

"I won't." I shove him hard, and he tightens his grip on me. "I messed up, ok?"

"Whatever. I don't care anymore."

"Leora - I messed up. Everything I wanted to say to you came out wrong. Please. Just listen. Don't say anything. Just listen."

I shake my head. He can talk all he wants. I don't have to listen to a word of it.

He's still holding me in his arms, he's even shifted his body so that his legs are wrapped around me too. I'm sitting in between his legs leaning up against his chest and I hate it.

He still smells so good.

"In the bedroom - I was trying to tell you that ever since we got married - I have been a complete asshole—"

"I know." I snap.

He sighs. "I didn't see what was right in front of me. I think I was too scared to see it. You came into my life like a tornado. Disrupting everything. But adding color and light and laughter to everything too. Then I treated you like total shit. I took you for granted - trying to hold on to my old life. But - I don't want that life anymore. And when you pulled away from me it hurt. I missed you."

He pauses, taking a breath. Waiting for me to say something but I stay quiet.

His words have caught my attention, but I'm too scared to misunderstand them.

I stay very still, sitting in his arms, up against his body.

"Leora - when you left - when I saw you on the cameras - it broke me. I knew I was the reason you left. And I don't blame you at all. It was my fault, and you had every right to do what you did - but I was trying to tell you it hurt me. It hurt me because I have fallen for you, and I really don't want to lose you."

I can't believe it.

I want to cry and laugh at the same time.

I want to kiss him.

I want him to kiss me.

But I can't move.

I'm terrified.

My heart is too scared to accept this.

"Leo - little kitten - please forgive me for hurting you. And please - give me a chance to fix everything. Give me a chance to show you how much you mean to me. I don't care how long it takes. I want to win you back. I won't stop trying. All I need is for you to give me a chance."

"Mas." I whisper, unsure of what will come out of my mouth next. Turning a little in his embrace I look into his eyes. I want to read them. I want to see what I can see in his gaze. I bite my lower lip. All I see is honesty. I see his pain, his desperation. It reflects my own back towards me.

I reach my hand up and touch his face.

I have never seen him being vulnerable and in this moment, he is more beautiful than ever before. Is heart is open, and he's taking a risk on me.

I lean forward, pressing my lips against his.

The kiss is slow and tender. I feel his hands wrapping around the back of my neck as he presses his mouth harder against mine.

It feels perfect. Intimate. Beautiful.

We kiss for ages, alone on the beach, listening to the waves as they lap against the sand in the dark.

Then I lean back and smile.

"I've been waiting for you to want me." I whisper.

"I've always wanted you. I was just too much of an idiot to know it. But when I think back - every moment with you - it was so obvious right from the start. From that kiss."

And in that moment, I know I love him - and I will take another risk on him. I will risk it over and over again - because he means everything to me, and I can't stop my heart from feeling the way he makes me feel.

CHAPTER TWENTY-SEVEN
Masaccio

We sit on the beach for ages. I don't want to let her go. I can't believe it took me this long to see the truth of it all. How beautiful her soul is - how perfect she is for me.

When the music from way down the other side of the beach goes quiet, I know the beach bar has closed. It's late.

"Let's go back to the villa and cuddle." I say, standing up and lifting her in my arms. I carry her, cradled against my chest, across the sand. She snuggles her face into my neck.

"You smell so good." She mumbles.

I look down at her, then kiss the top of her head.

Back in the villa I undress her, just enjoying how beautiful she is.

Then I lift her into the bed and wrap the blankets around her before I climb in next to her.

She lets out a deep yawn. I am also exhausted. The emotional toil of confusion - her tears - the relief of finding out the truth afterwards - it's enough to send me into a deep sleep.

I pull her back against my chest, her body curved perfectly against mine.

She wiggles against me, and I grin.

She really does feel amazing.

Letting out a soft sigh she closes her eyes, so do I, and we both drift off to a very peaceful sleep with the sound of the ocean singing to us in our dreams.

In the morning, I wake up wondering if I dreamt everything. But in my arms, sleeping peacefully, is the most beautiful girl in the world.

I smile as I pull her close to me, her head resting on my chest.

She stirs and mumbles in her sleep.

Then opens her eyes and sits up in shock.

"Hey. It's ok. It was just a dream—" I say, pulling her back down.

"No - actually - for a second, I was *worried* that it was just a dream. But it wasn't." She says.

She smiles as she closes her eyes again and runs her hand over my chest.

"I'm so cozy." She whispers.

Brushing my fingers through her hair my heart feels warm and full of love.

"Leo - can I take you out on a date? Our first *official* date."

She looks up at me with sleepy eyes. "I would love that."

"Good. I'll make the arrangements for tonight. You can go shopping today to buy something special to wear if you'd like?"

"I suppose if it is our very first date, I want to impress you." Her laughter drifts in the air and makes my heart even warmer.

"Everything about you impresses me." I whisper.

While Leora is out shopping, I want to plan something beautiful. Something she will never forget. Because tonight is where our relationship restarts. We get to start again and do it right this time. I am going to make up for every stupid thing I did or said - and from tonight - she will be the happiest girl in the world because I will make sure of it.

By five that evening I have arranged the most magnificent first date for her. One that will hopefully make her forget our rocky start.

Leora arrives back from shopping and walks into the little villa she booked for herself.

"Hello." She grins and steps close to me to wrap her arms around my waist.

"Hi beautiful. You can go get ready now. Then we can go."

"Oh - where are we going? Did you book us a restaurant?"

"Something like that. Just wear flat shoes - I mean this is a beach holiday." I grin.

"Is that the only hint you are going to give me?" she laughs as she carries her shopping bag towards the bathroom.

I am waiting for her out on the front deck of the villa. Admiring the drifting white clouds. When she steps out into the late afternoon sunshine my jaw drops open. She is wearing a fitted baby blue dress which hugs her curves in the most enticing ways.

She has gold strapped sandals on, and her toes are painted the same color as her dress.

"Baby girl - wow." I say, standing up and immediately dragging her against my body. She smells like wild vanilla and ocean salt. The perfect combination.

"Are you ready?" I ask, still holding her.

"I'm excited." She laughs.

Picking up the bag I have packed in preparation I sling it over my shoulder, hold out my hand to her and then lead her straight out onto the beach in front of the villa.

There is a small boat waiting for us.

I toss the bag into it, then lift her into it as well. She is grinning. "This seems like a little adventure - not a date."

"It's going to be an adventure." I smirk.

The little powerboat speeds through the water, sending a fine spray of ocean water into the air around us as it heads towards the yacht.

We park against the stern, and I lift her onto the swimming platform.

The sun will set in about an hour - and the chef has already laid out our dinner table on the top deck.

"Masaccio - this is incredible." She says, walking towards the dinner table.

"Mm. Not so fast. That's for later." I take her hand and pull her along behind me - to where the dive master is waiting for us.

"Hello, hello." He grins.

"Tony?" Leora says in surprise.

She glances towards me with a sharp look of hope shining in her eyes. "Are you going to dive with me?" she asks.

"Not just any dive - we are going on a night dive."

Her jaw drops open, and she jumps up in excitement.

Tony hands her some diving gear. "Sorry, your hair looks great, but it's about to get wet and salty." He laughs.

We dive into the water just as the sun sinks into the horizon, casting long beams of light across the surface of the water.

Tony has given us each an underwater light and we spend over an hour exploring the coral reef and the bright, beautiful sea life along it.

Our adventurous dive includes three different species of sharks which Leora is so eager about that she grabs my hand under the water so tightly it hurts.

But now, nearing the end of our dive, is the moment that I've been really nervous about this entire time. Swimming with sharks is nothing compared to the intense anxiety right now.

Leora is swimming at my side. I take her hand. "Come and look what I found in the coral." I tell her.

"Ok." She grins, pulling her goggles back down over her face.

We dive down following my beam of light - then I stop and point it at a small treasure chest I've left on the red coral. It's tiny.

Leora goes to pick it up. She glances back at me curious, confused.

Then she opens the lid and inside she finds a ring. She closes the lid again and swims back up to the surface.

"What is this?" She blurts out pulling her goggles off again.

"It's my great grandmother's ring. A family heirloom. I have kept it for years, waiting, wishing, but never believing that I would find the girl of my dreams."

"But - why is it—"

"Leora, little kitten, will you marry me?"

She screams with excitement and throws her arms around my neck, dragging me under the water while we both laugh.

"Yes, yes I'll marry you - again - um - I'll marry you." She shouts.

We swim back to the yacht and stand on the deck, water dripping off our bodies. I take the ring out of the tiny treasure chest and slip it onto her finger.

"Our first wedding was not something that we chose for ourselves. It wasn't even about us. But this time - it is going to be about only us and nothing else."

She stares down at the red rubies and diamond forming the shape of a rose on the gold band sitting on her engagement finger. "It's the most beautiful ring I've ever seen."

"It's very old. And unique." I say, pulling her up against my body, lifting her face with my hand wrapped about her jaw. Then pressing my lips against hers.

CHAPTER TWENTY-EIGHT
Leora

The first time I got married it was a whirlwind of people and chaos. It was a beautiful day, filled with the energy and noise of a thousand people - the second time I got married was very different.

I wake up in the beach villa alone, wondering where Masaccio has disappeared to.

I call his name, but there is no answer.

"Mas?" I wonder if he went for a run on the beach?

Getting out of bed, missing him already, I make myself a coffee and step out onto the front deck, watching the ocean.

A young girl walks up to me, carrying a big bag. She is grinning and has a bright look in her eyes.

"Leora - it's time to get ready."

She walks up the steps onto my deck.

"I'm sorry - who are you?" I ask in confusion.

"Masaccio is waiting for you. I am here to help you get ready."

She is pushy and bossy when she ushers me back into the villa, dropping the bag onto the sofa.

"Go shower and I will set it all up."

"Um - ok." I reply, completely confused about what is going on. But now that I know Masaccio is behind this, I'm feeling excited as well.

I shower. Luckily, I washed my hair the night before.

When I come back into the main area of the villa, the girl is standing there holding the most gorgeous lace white dress. Soft fabric that flows right down to the floor. Thin, delicate layers that will dance in the breeze.

"Is that?" I step forward and run my fingers along the lace patterns.

"It is your wedding dress." She smiles.

It takes me under an hour to get ready.

She curls my hair and braids it in a big loose braid down my back, pinning white flowers in all the way down and then placing a halo of white flowers on top. My make up is light, soft and natural. I am not even wearing shoes.

She gives me a single white lily to carry.

"You are ready." She pushes me towards the long mirror and staring at myself in the reflection I feel a lump forming in my throat.

I know I felt happy the first time I married Masaccio. I know I felt beautiful.

But nothing compares to what I feel right now.

The subtle, yet elegantly romantic style of this dress, the flowers dripping through my hair - the red rose ring on my finger.

My heart is so happy it feels like it might explode.

"Come on. It's time to go." She pulls the door open and ushers me out of the villa.

I can't stop smiling.

"You will follow this pathway," she points to a roped path, white, and red flowers threaded along the rope strung from pole to pole.

I turn to thank her, but she is already gone.

It is about no one else but us.

My smile is glowing as I follow the flowers towards where Masaccio is waiting on the beach.

He is standing barefoot at the edge of the water, the waters lapping at his feet, beneath a gorgeous pergola dripping with flowers.

Next to him is the man who will guide us through our vows.

With the salty ocean water kissing my feet, and my eyes locked onto my husband, I listen to the personal vows he has prepared just for me.

My heart is growing, warm and full of love for this man. I cannot get enough of him.

I want to wrap my arms around him and kiss him for an eternity.

But I wait. I let each moment of this beautiful ceremony etch itself into my memory because I want to recall it when I am old, wrinkled and lying next to Masaccio in bed each morning.

I want this to last forever.

"You may now kiss your bride."

The wind stirs my dress as I step closer to him.

He wraps his arm around my waist and dips me backwards as his lips press into mine.

I can smell the ocean, and his cologne. I can feel the heat of his body and the warmth of the sunshine. I can feel each beat of his heart against my chest.

His kiss is tender, but passionate. A kiss that will stay on my lips for all eternity. Just as he will stay in my heart.

When the ceremony is over the man leaves, and we stand alone under the flower pergola.

"Leora, I have bought that little villa. It's small, not what I would usually choose - but it means more to me than any other property I have ever bought because it is where we truly fell in love."

I shake my head and say. "You are crazy Masaccio." I giggle at his expression.

"We can come here whenever you want. And yes, I am crazy - crazy in love with you."

"Just as long as you know our love is not in a villa, or on a beach. I carry my love for you in my heart. It will always be there. No matter where in the world we travel. Who we meet. Where we sleep at night - my love for you is with me always."

"I know, little kitten. My love for you reaches to the edge of our universe - and then still goes beyond that. That is why words aren't enough to explain it. But I do want us to have a special place where we can visit - and even renew our vows every time we come here. Because I will marry you a thousand times across a thousand years. I love you - and I will always choose you, Leora."

He lifts me in his arms and carries me back to our villa.

He sits on the edge of the bed, and I climb onto his lap, pulling my wedding dress up over my hips.

I rock myself against him, feeling how hard his cock is.

I want him, more than I have ever wanted him before.

He pulls his pants open and frees his massive cock. Then he grabs my panties and tears them off me.

Sliding his cock inside me taunting me with the pleasure of it.

Then we rock together, moving like the ocean, back and forth with his hands on my hips and mine around his neck. I stare into his eyes and feel myself being pulled into deep pools of love.

His cock throbs inside me and my pussy begs for more. I want him to move faster, I want him to push deeper - but he doesn't. He continues his slow and steady thrusts, pushing and pulling my hips as I sit with my legs spread wide over his lap.

The pleasure builds, slowly, more intensely than I ever thought it could. Masaccio growls a deep, vibrating sounds that rumbles against me.

He is fighting for control. Fighting to keep his rhythm steady.

I giggle, thrusting my hips a little faster and he moans.

I think it's my turn to take control.

I wrap my fingers over his shoulders, holding onto him as I rock my hips faster, thrusting hard against him and pressing my weight down onto his cock so that he is buried all the way inside me.

He stops trying to control my movements, giving in to how incredible it feels.

I thrust forward and pull back and his cock slides in and out of me.

I cry out with each movement.

I can feel him getting harder by the second and my pussy is pulsing over his cock.

I can barely hold myself together. My entire body is shaking.

He grabs my hips, lifting me slightly, and starts fucking me so hard that I have to hold on even tighter.

His cock slams into me, over and over again. Until I am blinded by pleasure.

I throw my head back and scream his name as the tidal wave of my orgasm rocks through my body like a storm. It surges through me repeatedly.

Then I feel him explode inside me, gripping me tightly against him so he can push deep into me.

He collapses backwards onto the bed, pulling me with him.

We are both panting. Grinning and glowing with sweat.

He laughs and I know that laugh - full of mischief.

He lifts me in his arms and carries me out of the villa door, onto the sand - and right into the bright clear blue water of the ocean. In my wedding dress. I scream and pretend to fight against him - not that I could if I tried - and besides - the water feels incredible.

Floating in his arms in the salty sea. He pulls me against him and kisses me again.

"I love you, little kitten." He whispers.

"I love you, Masaccio. My husband."

About the Author

Hannah Rio is from a small town where she grew up reading romance books sent monthly by her book club. She developed a flair for crafting intricate love stories. She understands the delicate dance of heartbreak and joy. As a storyteller, she enjoys contemporary romances with strong, ambitious leading characters working through life's unexpected twists. Her female and male characters can make hearts flutter and eyes tear up. Her novels promise to bring readers back to continue events of new love and passion, secrets, surprises, painful memories, sassy and sweet, grumpy or good-hearted, and adventures with happy ever after endings.

Sign up to her newsletter here:

https://dl.bookfunnel.com/slno67x24w

- instagram.com/hannahrio2024
- amazon.com/author/hannahrio
- linkedin.com/in/hannah-rio-218707307

Also by Hannah Rio

BILLIONAIRES & BABY DADDY'S

Billionaire Baby Daddy Dilemma

Off-Limits Silver Fox Boss

MAFIA MEN

Vece Familia Series

Something Old

Something New

Something Borrowed

Something Blue

Printed in Great Britain
by Amazon